2

P E G

K E

B A A D

2
PEG
KE
BAAD

Nikita Lalwani

Srishti
PUBLISHERS & DISTRIBUTORS

Srishti Publishers & Distributors
Registered Office: N-16, C.R. Park
New Delhi – 110 019
Corporate Office: 212A, Peacock Lane
Shahpur Jat, New Delhi – 110 049
editorial@srishtipublishers.com

First published by
Srishti Publishers & Distributors in 2016

Acknowledgements

So you want me to thank you? I see!

Had I been 2 peg down while writing the stories, they might never have taken the form of a book. Hence, to start with, I appreciate my consciousness while being a part of fourteen magical journeys of my life through these stories. I am grateful to the almighty for letting me into this consciousness and making me appreciate and share the beauty of life with everyone through this book.

2 Peg Ke Baad is not a one man show. People whom I don't know and probably may never meet again, have contributed to the stories in more ways than one. A big thank you to all those happy strangers!

I am blessed to have parents to support me in all the good and bad phases of my life and would like to take this opportunity to thank them for just being there. Thanks to my siblings, especially my brother Aakash, for the constant encouragement and suggestions to keep me going ahead in life.

A special thanks to the person without whose support the book would have just been a thought – Ashish Bhawnani. You have been an amazing friend.

Thanks to my team – Tapan, Sana, Ishan and Ankur – for mentoring and nurturing my plans and ideas and helping me make it a reality.

Thank you Sakshi, Parth, Amit, Haifa, Atulit, Diwakar, Mahek, Ankita, Bobby uncle, Soma and half-conscious strangers for sharing their 2 peg ke baad stories.

I am glad to have support of Srishti Publishers and their team, especially the editors for covering my errors and making the stories look beautiful. Had it not been for you guys, things might have never worked so well. Thank you Saurav, for dressing up the book well, with all your patience.

Please consider the fact that I have a poor memory, just in case I failed to mention your name here.

Introduction

My mother always said, "After two pegs, nothing can go right."

But I feel the world's most interesting stories surface only after two pegs. So, here I bring to you my 'after two pegs' short story collection. The book includes stories in various genres from different people from across the world. The book does not encourage drinking alcohol in any way, though there is no denying the fact that every euphoria, high, dysphoria or unconsciousness of mind has brought us incredible events which at times have turned out to be life-changing. The stories are wrapped around almost anything that kicks the mind *2 pegs ke baad*!

A Walk With A Call Girl

◎

I have always wondered how it would feel to sleep with a prostitute. Definitely fun, but would kissing her with just the intention to get into her pants really be that great? As a man I know that one seeks more pleasure by cajoling someone and not just buying it right away. The more difficult it is to win yourself a good deal (or a good pair) of love making that is nowhere close to love, the more amazing it appears to be. Though the fact remains that any action is better than staying dry. It astounded me that kissing someone with no love or passion to win her would be satisfying.

It was a night with a prostitute; and it was nowhere close to what it may sound like. No, it wasn't the most elite sybaritic time I had with her. To be more specific, there was no sybaritic time at all, and yet it was a night I would always remember.

It was only when I met her that I realized that spending a night with a prostitute could also mean buying her a drink and some time to talk, and that could be worth more than those eleven minutes of pleasure bought for few clams.

✦

June 2011
Clarke Quay, Singapore

I was with four of my friends on the streets of Singapore city. The night was resplendent and ready to offer us the best of what it had. Singapore was the asserted destination for Subodh's bachelor's night celebrations. Aye! One of the five was soon to get hitched and so we chose Singapore to celebrate the remaining few days of his 'himself-hood'. Two in the group were twins – Aman and Ayan. Ayan was in a relationship which he claimed to be very serious about. Aman on the other hand was pretty much single, but at the same time too prudish to ask a girl out. All he needed was an introduction to manhood and Imran took the lead of being his mentor for the night. Everyone except Ayan was imperative to get some action that night.

Clark Quay is one of the finest dine and wine areas along Riverside in the city. We entered and it was like a street-walk mall. There were ladies of pleasure from every territory on the earth – Russia, Philippines, Brazil, Korea and God-knows-where-else. They were extremely inviting and all awaiting for our eyes. You sit-talk-buy them a drink and if that pleases you, you have grabbed yourself a treat. Although we were surrounded by them, nothing really came to descry. Subodh, the groom to be, though found a lady to his colt's tooth while the rest of us were not content with the crowd there.

We fled from that club. The best part about streetwalkers in Singapore is that despite the fact that they are available way cheaper than in India, they are elite in every sense. When you look at them you cannot judge whether they are contrivances to your desire for getting laid or an aristocrat lady! Each one has her own story, her own background and not everyone has been on sail through a tragedy. They are stark professionals, and the best part is that you don't even realize it.

Our next step-in was at Bricks, a night club in Hotel Hayat. Now, this was something, and although Clark is supposed to be one of the most bon ton clubs of the city, we found what we were looking for at Bricks. To begin with, it wasn't a mall. It was the one place where all your senses and your Indian intelligence might fail to decipher who's who.

Empirically speaking, and I mean it, this place was special. The girls around us were something else. Each one merited a "wow". Imran took the lead. We took our seats at a single side corner couch in the midst of the trans and tequila. Right then, my eyes caught a gilt-edged girl sitting four beer tables away, against the bar counter. She was wearing black, sitting with her legs crossed which ended with her red block heels. I am not sure if she was Russian, but one thing that I am pretty sure of – I had never seen a girl as elite and glamorous as her. I am short of words to describe her. She had a long slender neck that made her back glitter impeccably every time she turned. I couldn't hold back after that. Her glittering skin was no less than a wizard's spell that made my reluctance to approach her vanish. And so I did.

"Hi! Rihaan." I walked up to her but all I received was her cryptographic smile. She turned away leaving me puzzled.

"Can I buy you a drink, ma'am"? I tried again with the best of my manners.

"Sorry, I am not available," she said

"I am sure, but could we not just have a drink together?"

"Thank you very much, but my answer is still the same," she said.

I was bemused by her answer. What was she there for at all, and all alone? I went back to my seat and a few minutes later she surfaced in my conversation with Imran. We were baffled to find her sitting all alone. She looked like she was waiting for someone, but at the same time we were not convinced of her not being one of those working ladies. This time Imran gave it a shot.

"Sorry, I am not interested," straight and simple, she turned him down.

"What do you want? You tell us your best price and we are ready to give it," Imran offered.

"You can't," she grinned.

"C'mon, give it a try."

"It's the last time that I am warning you to walk away or I will call security."

An Indian waiter sneaked into the scene and whispered to Imran to get aside. Later he disclosed to us her decree and iterated though she was a professional, she was definitely not our treat.

The three of us sat with our jaws dropped looking at the blondes there. Few minutes later we watched a beefy shrimp in a black costume and lots of gild around his neck and wrists and teeth, walking in. He was one of the ugliest black (no offence) men I have ever seen and his built was humungous. He placed himself in a giant couch with a couple of ladies. An hour later, the blonde in the black dress, who had rejected the two of us, walked out with him.

Meanwhile Imran took it upon himself to find bait for Ayan. They finally found the right girl. Imran mentioned Ayan's reticent demeanour and within an hour they walked out into the sinful land. On enquiring from the Indian waiter, we learned that the colossus under all that gold was a whale of some syndicate running in Singapore. He walked out with two girls on either side and each was paid a lakh for a night. We got the explanation to why she had said that we couldn't pay her price.

The night was turning gloomy. We wasted a lot of good time while others sheered into someone's pants. We sat pointlessly ogling at the ladies getting booked one by one.

I walked up to the rock band that was playing at one end of the pub. The bass was flawless. There is not much difference between getting laid and playing drums; the harder you hit, the better the cords revert. Waving our hands with the crowd, we enjoyed a pint over a couple of compositions. I was almost 2 pegs down by then and halfway down to the beer in my hand when I noticed a girl in a black dress by my side. She too was enjoying the music – although not as much as I was. We shared a casual look at first. She was beautiful. I couldn't keep my eyes off her. Another track scratched in and this one ended up with us sharing a smile. I gently raised a toast while I was still under the enigma whether or not I should approach her. I was just a bit tipsy when I walked back to my couch. By then I could see Imran sharing his couch with a lady. I took a few sips from my pint and eased myself on the couch. While I randomly checked around the crowd in the bar, the girl in the black dress turned to me.

"Hello, may I?"

"Sure," I moved in.

"Hi, I was observing you and it seems you have been left all alone by your friends."

I grinned looking at Imran. "That is true," I retorted.

"So would you like to buy me a drink?" And she dropped me an inkling. For a second I was surprised, for I haven't been around a girl who was way better looking than any of our Bollywood actresses and models and supposedly a prostitute. Well, there was yet a lot to learn in Singapore. I got her a drink while we sat and enjoyed some waffles over every quaff.

"Why do all girls go for a martini?" I asked.

"Well, I don't know about others but this was the last drink my boyfriend ordered before his last breath. So, this drink means a lot to me."

"Oh, I am sorry. What exactly happened to him?"

"Seriously! I was kidding. My ex-boyfriend is hale and hearty in Brazil. I can't believe you bought that," she chuckled and so did I silently at my folly. "Maybe it's because of the hierarchy."

Then she told me the flakiest story behind the statement about why all girls prefer martinis. I am a bit foggy about the details, so let's skip that part.

We talked for almost two hours and none of us was in any way ennui with all talk and no action – yet. There was something about her that attracted me. Not that she was the most beautiful girl in the room – there were many of her kind whose sleek legs windowing from in between the slit of their skirts were enough to create magic – but this one was different. She asked me if I wished to make a move to the bedroom but I rather enjoyed talking aimlessly with her, holding a drink in my hand and looking into her eyes. Not that I was looking for a straight nineties-fashioned romance, but more than anything, I just enjoyed the simplicity of that moment. Her perfume was inviting. I told her that I couldn't resist her fragrance. It cajoled me to ask her which brand she was wearing.

"Victoria's Secret," she answered.

"It's irresistible, I must say. I would like to buy one for my girlfriend."

"So you have a story back in your town?"

"Not really, I had once, but she's married now. This is with reference to a future situation…if any."

It was four in the morning and she asked me if I was interested to take her to my room, but I preferred chatting with her instead. Strangely, she too wished to continue the long meaningless conversation which would veer to not-so-meaningless later on. I had a few sips of my drink and was all upbeat. A few minutes of silence and I saw her texting someone. I asked her whom she was texting.

"You seem restless...anything wrong?"

"No, no, we have a circle of prostitutes and my friends are asking if I am hooked yet. I am just..." she said as she typed furiously into her BBM "...just telling them that it's not my call for tonight."

"But I am surprised how a girl as ravishing as you got left, no rather stuck 'talking' to a guy like me."

"Well, I am kind of enjoying this moment – all talk, no play. Dude! Even I need a break from work."

"Of course."

She was amazing, the most amazing prostitute I have ever met. Well, not that I keep seeing prostitutes. This was just the third time I was with one, but I had no clue that a six feet tall and fair blonde would keep me wide awake and interested in getting to know her. Hell yeah!

"Why don't you tell me why you are apparently stuck 'talking' to me?" she tossed my question right back at me.

"I couldn't really find a girl who matched my height! Even if I did I don't wish to walk out of this wonderful conversation I'm having with you for some eleven minutes of fun."

Man! She had an enticing smile. The bar was emptying out and only a few like us were left behind. We decided to move out. She carried her shimmering silver heels in one hand and a pint of beer in the other while we walked alongside the streets of Singapore city at four in the morning.

"So, how do you happen to be here?" I initiated

"You mean here with you?"

"No, I mean, here in Singapore."

"Oh, you mean how did I end up becoming a pro?" She took a sip of her pint and shrugged her shoulders. "I am basically from Philippines. Year 2004, the December tsunami turned our lives around. My dad lost a lot of business in that – almost everything. So we moved to Vietnam and I came to Singapore in search of a job and now I am here. That's it."

"So, your family is aware of…"

"No, no. They think I work in a 24x7 store here. It has been six months that I have been doing this. I visit home once a year and as long as I can send enough money back to them, it is all okay to me."

I was taken back for a moment. There was an uncomfortable pause but she broke it saying, "Aw, c'mon, I am really okay. I mean at first I did feel bad, I'll be honest. In fact, I was devastated for the first few days as if I had no worth, but then everything turned out to be alright. No big deal!

We walked a few more steps ahead, shared some more incidences, enjoyed a few more smiles and experienced some deep sighs. In no time it was seven and it was time for Tina's shift to end. We watched the sunrise together and exchanged each other's contact details.

I told her it had really been nice being with her. She wondered if I would be coming back that night to the bar again. Unfortunately we were to leave that very day. I hugged her tight, and she snuggled into my arms. Those few seconds felt like eternity and none of us wished for the moment to end. I held her face in my hands and put my lips on hers. That was the sweetest kiss she had ever received, she told me. I don't know whether that was her professional manners or her honest review, but to me, it was definitely the sweetest and yet the most meaningless kiss that I have ever had.

My Last Painting

©

L ife. Here is a thing about life: it might make you believe that you have everything in control, but the truth is that nothing really is.

I'll never forget that night – how could I, it was my last. It was raining outside as I sat by my window checking the tiny droplets streaming down it. There was no other sound in the room but of the pitter-patter of the rain. Fortunately it was raining otherwise the place was as silent as a graveyard. The clock struck 11.00 p.m. as I reached out for the Teacher's bottle lying in my wardrobe. Sana and I had bought it sometime back. Sana happened to be my flat-mate who barely resided here. During the day we never saw each other, being busy at our own work places. Eventually she started dating a guy from her office and then I hardly saw her at our place during the night too.

It has been almost two-and-a-half years since I have known Sana. I moved from Korba to Pune, looking for nothing but job satisfaction. Soon I learned one thing – there is nothing like 'job satisfaction'. Not unless you are ready to settle at your target.

Once you get a job you yawp about being paid less, and two months after every increment you may seem to be where you always wished to be, but after that you will soon find a point to yawp about, again.

In my case, job satisfaction was more about being able to do what I wish rather than winning a good pay. You cannot escape the former. So at times, I'd rather wine about it than whine.

That night I chose the same. With a box of ice, a bottle of whiskey and a letter in my hand, I sat down leaning on the sliding window. The letter in my hand was a resignation letter signed in the name of Ananya Jethi – that's me.

I slowly and gently poured the drink into a glass, added some water, dropped a few ice cubes into it and took a long sip as I gazed at the moon from my window. It was a full moon night, though the clouds passing the moon made it hazy at times. My mind was full of a million thoughts. It was difficult to look at the moon; the thoughts within me made it seem hazier to me. I turned back to reading the words in that letter again.

Coming back to job satisfaction, which I soon discovered was another phrase for a switcher, got me into a website company in Pune. At first I started as a writer. Not that I was really into writing, but somehow they happened to like my blogs and called me. There were just two things I am still passionate about – wine and painting. Writing was not really different from painting; it just involved words instead of colours. Anything creative attracted me, so I decided to hop on the job offer. In no time I was the copywriter of that company. My bosses liked me and they liked my work. And this is the myth we lead ourselves to believe when working with a creative agency.

I made myself a second peg.

So you have no connection with this company...at least emotionally? We need you here...I need you here...your confidence is commendable...you put your talent in the ink...you will soon be the chief editor here...do you wish to leave?

I remember how things were to me then. Chief Editor. It sounded great, but there is a thing with creative agencies: they want your talent, but they're not sure of whether or not they want you. And as far as Kiaan was concerned, he would go to any length to keep me backing him.

Kiaan was my boss but things had really been different between us. I came in contact with him when the company was reshaping itself. It was not really a boss-employee relationship that we shared; we were more like friends. He liked me; at least that's what I gathered from what he used to say then. It was those six months that we had totally lived our lives with each other. It was probably the best time of my life. He called me all the time and soon we were dating. Everything was going good until the day he stopped taking my calls. I don't really have an answer to it till date. But it was simple for him to explain: 'Why should I call you every day?'

He had responsibilities and things do not stay the same way forever; nothing stays the way it is.

I have no pent up angst for Kiaan. He had his own reasons and I respect them. He had never given me his word so if I ended up expecting too much, it was my own fault. I overlooked everything and tried focusing on my career.

Everything was settled. Although at times I did find myself unable to resist, in which case I ended up calling him. But he never responded to any of my calls. With every call that went unanswered, I was left wondering what wrong I had done. Was I of no use to him now? Just six months and he was done? Were all those words he had uttered just words to keep me in his firm? Well, I was stuck; not because I was hoping for a promotion through him, but because I was too timid to walk away from him.

I was two pegs down already. I made myself a third one, 90 ml neat and swilled it in one go. The latency of the mind eventually reduced. It was easier to look at the moon now. It was a little less visible from behind the rushing clouds as I peered on it for the last time, reminding me yet again of how infidel life is.

Sunshine, you look like sunshine in white...when you smile there is a glitter in your eyes...I am in love with your smile...

...and I made myself another one.

They say, "Whine a little and you will feel better", I say, "Wine a little and you will feel much better." Anyway, I had no one around but myself to whine a little to. I still had the letter in my hand. It was my resignation. This time I wanted to whine about it, because I had no one reason and no fair reason for bringing that up.

For a moment I wished Sana was around. I really wished to ramble a little about what I was going through. I wished to wrangle with Kiaan like I used to, holding his shirt which made me grab nothing more but his attention and that look. I miss that look. I miss him. With every little tiff in the office there was a kiss to calm me down and so I came up with a new tiff just to make him cuddle me every time. It was hard to let him go, and harder to see him flirt with other women while he was still there in front of me.

Presently I was jobless, loveless and had no one to talk to. I just wanted to let myself out to someone. I was burning within. I was four pegs down and it wasn't working.

I put away the letter and went in. I took out a canvas. It is a lot easier to sing out loud when you are a singer, or write down if you are a writer. All your sorrows would soften down to a beautiful creation. I was a painter and the best tools I found to communicate then were my paint brushes and the old colour tubes which were almost squeezed empty.

Swaggering towards the balcony I set myself in front of the canvas. I swirled the oil with the rest of the paints on the tray and started painting. I didn't know what I was going to paint, like most of the times. I just allowed myself to move with the flow of the colours and feelings because only they knew what best they may wrench out of me.

All I was aware of was that I was using purple. It was his favourite colour, but it was not the reason why I had picked it. I recalled everything that had happened to me in the last one month.

Why are you creating all this fuss? Did I tell you something? Any promises that I made? What is the whole big scene all about?

She is Rukhsar, company's new copywriter...of course she will be under you to learn how we work... Rukhsar, please inform Ananya of the changes I discussed with you...Why don't you ask Rukhsar, she knows it all...Leave it Ananya, you won't be able to do it.

I didn't realize how one thing led to another and within no time I was a junior again. I had to take orders from those who were once supposed to be under me. And I didn't understand why and how quickly it had happened. Soon I was brushing in some yellow. Mixing my tears into the paints, I made a rough stroke across the canvas, again with no blip of what I was painting.

There were times when I thought about leaving the job. I had better offers too, but god knows what kept me glued there. I was so used to Kiaan being around me that nothing else really made sense, not even being paid more and respected more. My parents were concerned about me having a good job, to be able to draw a fine bio data for me. My constant switching of jobs was annoying them and so was my disinterest in marriage. I could think of marrying no one else other than Kiaan. I knew he would never do it and he never said anything about it, but in my mind I still hoped of asking him.

> *I'll never get married…or maybe I will…I don't have any plans. I know what women are like and what all of them want…probably, I have lost all faith in marriage…I can see how alike we both are: our thoughts, our beliefs… you are the kind of girl I would like to sit with watching just your eyes…I really love talking to you…I haven't talked this much to anyone in ages.*

We talked for eighteen hour in a day. Why in the world would I not expect him to like me the way I did? He made me believe in his words. And maybe since all the women in his life talked him into a relationship or dating, I hoped my stepping ahead would work.

I took a mouthful of my drink and looked at the painting. It was a lady. She looked beautiful, not really like me but her eyes said a lot. My eyes at that moment were just filled with tears – reflecting red, orange, green, blue and many more colours enclosing a gamut of my feelings within.

I wiped my tears with my hands covered with paint. What kind of life did I have at present? The person whom I loved had signed my resignation and would never like to hear again from me. I didn't have a job, and my parents had lost their faith in me. They thought that I was a loser; I won't deny that because I actually was.

I know that things will change. Nothing stays the same. I will eventually get a better job, will meet new guys and will get married, but I will never have Kiaan in my life. I was not ready to live with that idea. I don't blame him; he had his own reasons. He wanted to focus on his career, had been in more disturbed relationships than successful ones, and probably has lost all his faith in marriage or even women. Maybe it was me – to not ask him out in the first place, to not continue dating him more like a woman than a girl, to be coy, to afoot my ego, to resign, to not compromise...

I didn't know even then that it had not been enough. I picked up the brush and painted tears pouring out of her eyes. Now she looked quite like me.

"This is my resignation letter."

"Seriously, what are you up to? This is the most critical time for the company and it needs you more than anyone here. I am not signing this. C'mon! This company needs you. I need you!"

"Why do you need me when everything has been taken care of by Rukhsaar and Sheena and everyone else? I had been doing all the elbow greasing and they have been taking all the credit."

"Here is a new assignment for you. If you nail it, I promise you an increment."

That was a project worth a lakh and the increment I received was a measly two-and-a-half thousand, for then he had not said about drawing a margin for himself. I believed that.

Rukhsaar will be accompanying me to the award ceremony, I want you to stay here for next week's meeting...Sheena will be taking up the next assignment, you may help her if you want.

There is a thing with art – any art – the way a horny person feels after receiving an orgasm. At first the fiery urge for that thing and the very next moment the feeling of being free as if all they ever wanted was that very moment. An artist feels the same once he is done painting his emotions on the canvas. All the urges are satiated, all the feelings are expressed, and the eagerness is calmed. I took the last quaff from my glass and threw it on the floor.

One of the pieces shining at me was chosen. One sharp slit on my left wrist and the job was done.

"I can't work here anymore."

"Again? What is the matter with you? Increment, is it?"

"I am done. Just that."

"Ananya, there is so much here that only you can do."

"I have made up my mind. Here is my resignation."

"I thought you always asked me before making up your mind. I see, so you have really grown up."

"Maybe I should have a long time back."

"If this is what you want – here is your resignation letter approved," Kiaan held the letter to me with those words and left slamming the door behind him.

There was blood all around me; I fell on my knees, weeping. But I was not sad, not even for once. As I bled, all the emotions, all the pain and all the memories oozed out with the blood. After a very long time I was relieved. I was sitting surrounded by my own blood, watching my painting. It was definitely not my best till date. I had been a far better painter than that. Besides, the lady in the painting was crying, and the one outside of it was satiated.

Only then I realized that I did not sign the bottom of the painting. I reached out to pick up the brush with my right hand and the canvas with the left one. *Ananya* – I signed there. When I moved a step back, I was amazed to see what I had just done to my painting unintentionally. I smiled at it as this was my best work so far. While holding the canvas from the top I had accidently bled over my painting, and as the blood ran down it, it seemed to be coming out from the lady's eyes. I fell back looking at my last painting as my eyes shut slowly.

Now she looked exactly like me.

What Happens in Banaras...
Stays for a Lifetime

©

They say, "You can take a Banarasi out of Banaras but certainly not Banaras out of a Banarasi".

It's December 2014 and I am back in the city of Ghats – to the city of indispensable plinks of bells, chiming from across the temples, and the resounding 'Har-Har Mahadev' in every lane you cross. It was one of the abodes of the Hindu gods, but to me and all of us at BHU, Banaras was more than that.

It is time for us to asseverate that we have been technically, academically and morally screwed by one of the best institutes in the country – the Banaras Hindu University (BHU). Though a very few of us could make it on the Big Day, I was one of the thirty out of the batch of a hundred students to show up on the convocation day.

Right from the railway station to the BHU campus, there are two unavoidable smokes that cannot skip your olfactory nerves – of the *dhoop* and the weed – neither beneficial to the environment.

Entering the campus was a celebration in itself. Back at Bhopal, where I belonged, when I talked of life in Banaras, not even the pup beside would care to listen. And there was that feeling, the one you get while reading Munshi Premchand's books, or while watching Anurag Kashyap's movies. I was getting it again as we were brought to the ingress of the campus, dancing on the beats of drums with colour all over our face and garlands across our neck, as a real Banarsi would be welcomed.

Being a part of the BHU alumni, you are nourished with grass. Nothing else but weed and beer! Before getting into IIT, if I sit and recall my life, it was surrounded by the three mistakes I made: Physics, Chemistry, Mathematics. Nothing else existed. I had no real friends, nor did I remember playing pranks or had anything even close to what could be cherished as an affair. All I had were books and all that I knew was that I had to get into an IIT.

Back at the campus ingress, the farewell banner read, 'It's One Big *Joint* that Binds Us'. You pretty well know what that joint really was.

In the evening, we were out on the *ghats* to attend the seven o'clock clock *aarti*. We listened to the holy prayers chanted in the name of river Ganga first and then for Lord Shiva. The pundit in white dhoti stepped forward to offer us the aarti.

Banaras speaks to you through her ghats. We found one of our favourite places to sit on: the stairs on the river bank as we listened to the sound of aarti coming from behind the temple. *Diyas* floated on the river and from every direction all that could be heard was the holy chanting. Banaras was the same and nothing seemed to have changed in all these years. Not a bit. It was just the same.

Life here even surpasses Newton's first law of motion, which says, 'Every matter continues to be in a state of motion unless an external force is applied to it'. In Banaras, no external force is enough to move the city from its state of tranquil. The curve never shifts up or down. This is where you may stand still and look into yourself.

In Banaras, you may not find life moving, but definitely the life that exists within you is in a flux. Artists come from across India to find a muse for their pictures; the lads at every step chewing *paan* or *gutka* are back by six o'clock in the evening from work, the pundit in white dhoti and orange kurta chanting aarti at the same hour everyday and the saints taking dips in the water – these are all the people who make up the ancient town.

It was six years ago when I had first come here. It seemed like another day of my first year at college. Engineering had surely given me a lot to be able to stand ahead of the world, but what Banaras has given me is more than what can be summarized in words.

Back at school, I remember being a completely different person than what I discovered I was at Varanasi (yes, that's how tourists spell it). What I remember of my school days is that I had no friends, no girl friends, no teacher I had flirted with (even though I found some of them quite interested in me), there were no boy talks regarding girls, cricket or to-to. While guys of my batch were planning to plant bombs in the girls' washroom during recess, I used to be busy solving math problems with my juniors. Even though most of them were girls, and I often blushed in the name of some, I never gave enough heed to anything apart from my books. I am hardly in touch with anyone from school presently, because I never talked to people about anything other than the course.

On the day of my results, when I found out that I had not scored enough to get into IIT the first time, I thought of committing suicide. To me it was the end of life, end of myself and the end of all that I had ever wished for.

At around ten at night, with a joint and few pints of beer, we would sit on the ghats, watching a body being cremated by the side of the Holy Ganga. Banaras is one of the most auspicious Hindu lands for the cremation of dead bodies. I took a long fag of the *ganja* in my hand. The diyas floating on the river glimmered on the silent river and they seemed to be talking to each other. The tantric around the body chaffed their hands over the consummating wood.

While the body burns on one side, you see a *tawaif* or a call girl dancing wearing her *ghungroos* in the celebration of the freedom of another soul from this world

I took in my first quaff.

It felt like I was back where life begins – like the popping of a bud, the rising of a ray down from the zenith and to me, the first year at college.

There were three things that Banaras had taught me. To Give. To Love. To Live.

To Give

IIT is a bitch. At times you're almost tempted to give up but Har-Har Mahadev, I would say to thank God for my stay in Banaras where I was taught to give away rather than give up. I used to be the topper of my class until my school days, but things were not the same here. I was a five-pointer, and that means someone whose existence is not even considered by the teachers. I managed to scrape through every session and I gave two whoops in Hades about not scoring enough in the practical tests. We have always considered practical exams being girls' bowl of ice-cream; they topped them, no matter what. And if you are an engineer, you'd know why I said that.

I was, however, an honest student. I never considered cheating during theory exams, even if it meant consistently scoring really low marks. Unless the sneak peep into the girl's paper sitting beside you and asking the beginning of an answer was considered cheating. I had a problem with those bringing chits to the exam hall – that was the real thing. Peeking into someone's copy still required one's efforts to write the rest of the answer, so it could not count as 'real' cheating.

Therefore, I used to give away my marks to support the cause of honesty. I knew that I blurted technical terms and hardly smiled during the viva, but was the less considered candidate being more of a testosterone driven machine. I learned to give away my scores there as well for a long time.

But there had to come an end to my silence. I deserved better scores and they did not tip you with extra rasagullas during the mess lunch for being honest, anyway. So I decided I would not give away anymore.

For the next four semesters, I brought along notes to the exam hall; some in my pocket, some in the pencil box, a few inked on my hand, on the eraser and behind the admit card as well. Three semesters I scored well. But Banaras was not done with teaching me about giving away. Two more exams to go in the fourth semester, and I was caught red-handed in the middle of the third one.

I could not breathe. Prof Mannapalli had called me to the staff room. I stood silently in front of him, looking down at my shoe laces. Mannapalli looked at me through his glasses.

"I did not expect this from you. You have let my confidence in you down. I used to think that you weren't one of those students. You do have an innocent face," Mannu said and I felt as though I had screwed his daughter. I also thought had I really known about my innocent looks, I would have used them better.

"You are one hell of a useless, spoiled brat. Students like you are a blot on the face of BHU. One of the worst students I have ever had in my career..." he continued and my face lifted up at every sentence from my shoe laces to his shoe laces and then to his neck tie.

Worst student ever – really? And as I questioned myself, I unknowingly looked straight into his eyes.

"What? What are you looking at?

"I am not the worst student, Sir. I have scored well before," the vexed bastard raised his voice in pride.

"Do not think that you will be walking away under my surveillance. No one does that under my nose. You are a shame to this university and I will make you pay for this attitude. Mind well!" Mannu warned me through his double spherical glasses and wavering moustache.

And when Mannu said 'mind well', you've really got to mind well. He could ruin anything. More importantly, I was to leave for Barcelona for a summer internship the next month and had my visa application date in a few days. Mannu was required to give me an NOC for the same. But even if I escaped this one by forging an NOC, the news would be telecast overnight to my dad. That would be worse than being telecast on Star Plus; at least you had the Engineering students skipping that channel. My dad would have made sure that even the chai-wala in that corner of the street would know about what I had done in the exam. So Mannu's reprimand really meant a big deal to me.

Besides, he had already made it clear that I wouldn't be allowed to appear for the next exam.

I did not sleep the entire night and while watching the diyas blinking halfway to meet each other, gathered some hope to cajole Mannu to let me take the tests ahead. For the first time I felt that BHU had let me down. I didn't mind Mannu's fury at me, I deserved all of it, but not being called the worst student. I knew that he really, really meant it.

The next morning I pleaded, cried and now that it was acknowledged, used my innocence to persuade Mannu. Prof Mannapalli finally allowed me to score more than 60% in the next two tests and assured my release from the bad omen.

I gave it my best shot and had my summers enjoying Swiss chocolate and the ladies. By then I had given away my marks, my shame and my pride.

To Love

It was during my second year at college when I met this interesting girl, Manika. She was a friend at first and I do not remember when I developed feelings for her. But then why not; she was hot, she was intelligent (a little), and she was hot. That's pretty much it to make you feel lucky.

I liked her very much and all my friends had started teasing me. Meanwhile, my roommate Gupte was also seeing her. Initially, we held the phone for long hours in the night, but only I did so with a lot of feeling. Gupte turned out being a good friend of hers and before I could confront him, I learned that the two were dating each other.

Over *malai chaap* at Pehalwan's shop, I tried persuading Gupte about Manika. He knew how much I liked her and yet was seeing her. There was no big spat over her since Gupte and

I were very good friends, but somewhere we had begun to drift apart. We didn't talk much, didn't play squash together, and didn't go to watch movies in IP mall together anymore. The only time we were back to the 'bhai' phase was over a joint of weed.

I realized over time that it wasn't really my love for Manika that was holding me back, but the ego of losing a girl to my own friend. So I stood firm, and so did Gupte. Until the day when we both discovered that she had been going out with a third guy. We were torn, but at the same time nettled when we found out who the guy was. It was a massacre – rather a mephitis. He smelled bad, and even if he was the last guy in the college, no girl would ever go out with him. Plus, he never got a job, so the two of us were pleased to find out what we had been ditched for; peanuts, even when it came to the real thing. And like they'd say in Banarasi – the *bhaukal* (studs) were back.

That is when I learned how to love for real: not a girl, but my own friends. The 'bros before hoes' only hit my head right then and made me believe in the fact that in a lifetime, a bro can always find you a great hoe, but a hoe may take away your best bro.

To Live

Whether or not have you lived in Banaras, even if you have accepted it for a second, it will call you back again. Living in Banaras in itself was euphoria despite the fact that it took us a lot many fags to learn that. Our routine had us to study for twelve hours, play squash for two hours and stay in trance for the remaining ten. But there were few who did not let the remaining ten hours into their lives, or into their rooms. MAKKUs – the Madras Andhra Karnataka Kerala Union. To them, the rest of

India did not exist, or even if it did, it was during exams for a photocopy. They never considered anyone friends. And so did we, the remaining Indians.

Siddhant, Gupte, Anurag and I happened to rope in all the good and the bad for a drag. One of the few great things about Banaras was that weed was easily available at any paan corner, and even the saints dragged a big puff in the name of Har-Har Mahadev.

'Bob Marley – *hum na marey*' was what was written outside Sid's room.

We used to sit for long hours in Sid's room, making out with marijuana. The only problem was Subramanniam, Sid's roommate. Subramanniam was a teacher's pet and the warden's cat who would meow into the warden's ears even if his roommate farted, which made us to intently smoke our worries and assignments by his bed.

We made some adjustments in their room to make sure that Subbu was equally a part of the game. We would make sure that he was asleep and sealed the room to stop the smoke from getting out. The air cooler in their room was placed in front of Subbu's face and all that we fagged would be released into it. While we smoked one marijuana joint each, Subbu got four joints at once. None of us was ever in a state to find out what exactly happened with him every time, but we were sure the baby enjoyed the game subconsciously.

Banaras has taught me a lot many things: too many to summarize in Give-Love-Live, and too many that I am grateful for. It made me write my first poem, it taught me sharing; it taught me to care about little things in life; gave me some balls to walk up to girls, some more to walk up to my professors; made me stress-less when I didn't bathe for a week, brought me out from Paulo Coelho to take a look at Gulam Ali's compositions and made me quite a desi.

I opened another pint watching the burning flames around the body. A man with a wooden rod would hit hard on the head of the body. Our skull is tough and requires external effort to be brought down to a state where it would burn, but as per Hindu mythology, it is where the soul resides and it takes time for it to get released through the body. In tow with the 'tat-tat-thaiyee-thaiyee' in the distance from where the departure of the soul was cherished, the skull popped off, as though the body had fended it off. The soul was freed into the miasma, off into the air to another life. It is only then that you realize the fragility of a human body. We spend our entire lives whimpering about it and fail to realize the importance of the soul that lies within it, which meant so much more than being an IITian.

How We Got Married

Ⓒ

I am sitting in front of a mirror dressed in a *sherwani* and looking at the *yummy* dish in front of me. I wonder if tonight will be the last order for this dish, as after tonight it will be taken off the menu. The dish will be enjoyed by just one of its million contenders for the rest of his life, and practically for next fifty years. What will happen to the dish? Will it turn stale? Will it lose its taste? Will it be considered for the menu again?

(Spilling the beans: it wasn't all about the dish – it was about me, Parth, who is to be the groom tomorrow. Tonight happens to be my last night as a bachelor.)

I parry away from the mirror and turn to the bottle of Absolut Vodka on my dressing table. For a moment even the bottle seems to be joking with me. *Yummy Dish, your time is over! Grab a shot from me and get on the ground.*

I turned away from the bottle to walk out of the door, then walked back to the dressing table, made myself a vodka shot and swigged it down my gut. It felt better now! *And looks like you are going to need a lot more than that from now on.* Miss Absolut.

Marriage. We wait all our lives for this day. We begin when we strive for good grades in school so that we may get into a good college, strive for good grades at college so that we get a good job, strive at the nine to nine job so that we may get a promotion, and with the first promotion comes the first car at the cost of an EMI and a goodie-two-shoes wife at the total cost of the car. In fact, in a way, the wedding night turns out to be the happiest for most guys; most guys who never got a chance to discover themselves in Thailand. But for other guys, it takes a number of diazepams every day to make sure we walk down the aisle.

One year ago, Itarsi Railway Station

I woke up to the bedlam of 'chai-coldrink-thanda-garam'. I looked at my watch. It was ten in the morning, and we were still a few hours away from Bengaluru. I climbed down from my berth and widened my eyes to the mirror that reflected an uncouth version of me. Dark circles ran down my drooping eyes and my hair was long enough to be tied into a braid. I yawned and took a seat reaching into my pocket for my cell phone. It had been switched off for more than twelve hours now. Twelve missed calls and twenty-four messages – each wanting to know where I was and if I was fine.

I typed my first and last text to my sister Roopali saying that I was fine and requested them not to try tracking me. I sent another message that said: *miss you, my cell phone will be switched off.* The latter was not for Roopali. I switched off my cell phone and sat back looking at the strangers on the platform: the girl with long hair holding a blue hand bag was hugging a guy before she got on the train. The two were looking at each other and held hands until the train signalled to a start. The guy kissed her on the forehead and fended her off. The train started moving and they waved at each other until the last sight. It was us. I closed my eyes and all I could see was us. It was me and her at the station the last time we saw each other. She had given me a small peck on my cheek and hugged me tight as though she knew that there would never be a second time. My eyes were filled with tears and so was my mind with so many questions to be answered. There's a dark and empty space where I found myself standing then, and there has been no escape from there ever since. I wept and wept because that was all I could do. All I needed was to see her.

Six years ago, I could never imagine that six years down the line this would be me: helpless and daunted to face my own family and friends. I never knew that there would come a time when I would need to escape from my own parents and hide from my own friends. And escape not to some place like Goa, but to the love of my life. I never ever imagined I would use the phrase, 'the love of my life'. But love hits you when you least expect it.

Back in college, when I was in my third year of MDS, Paedodontics from VKDS College, Bengaluru, my life was pretty simple; simpler than anyone could imagine. Despite the most complicated things that could ruin anyone's PG life – thesis submissions, lecture dissertations, lamenting kids and their groaning parents, the weekly seminar besides the constant hammering by one's guide – life was yet way too easy for me and my friend Hrishabh.

Hrishabh was my junior cum flat mate cum best friend. No matter what life would throw at us, we'd live through it. We woke up late in the morning, dry cleaned ourselves with eau du toilette, attended college, gave a random speech in the seminar which the teachers happened to like most of the time (and if they did not, then I made sure they'd like something in me). Most of the time a smile would do the job. Back home, Hrishi and I would sleep till it was dark in the evening, then take a round around the city on my vintage bike and grab home some beer and then settle down to watch *Game of Thrones* and *Prison Break* until midnight. Occasionally we'd pick a book for the next day's seminar over few more beers and a pack of cigarettes and would fag the rings till four in the morning. That was our routine.

He was single, I was single, life was simple. There was no mushroom cloud or strangling belt of gooey romance around my neck. I dated girls – a lot of girls – one girl from each batch, but by God's grace I never had to shuffle my routine for any of them. I had always been blessed with pretty and understanding girls. If they needed to spend time with me, they would come to my place. If I needed to spend time with them, they would again come to my place and everything would be in place. They would talk, I would watch my serials. They would bring food, we would eat, and we both would be happy in the end.

I never felt the need to take out extra time for girls, nor did it take me any extra effort to get into their pants. There was no hot shot from the college whom I had not dated. After five years of my graduation and two years of the three from my PG, I had had enough of it. Most of the time, my juniors hovered around me to get their records approved or good grades in the practical exams or to get advice during exams since the teachers were on good terms with me. Seniors talked to me because I was notoriously famous and that made it intriguing to them, but no one had any intention to bind up with me. Good for me though, because I considered one girl for one trip of the fourth-yearly trips.

Only once during college did I feel that I was in love. It was in the second year of my under-graduation. She was a year senior to me and things had gone way too serious between us. However, she couldn't find a future in our relationship and got married to someone else.

And I got to be a brat yet again, but not for too long. Who knew then that this yummy dish was going to be all served at once?

Bangalore Railway Station, 10.00 p.m.

I had finally reached my destination. I switched on my cell phone and there were forty-eight unreturned calls and a few messages waiting for me. I opened my call log and hit a number,

"I am here; my phone would be switched off after this. I am heading to your place, need to see you soon… love you," I said in a quivering tone and hung up. I switched off my phone and got down from the train.

One year ago, VKDS College, Bangalore

Have you ever felt the tingles when you look at someone, someone special? The feeling that everything has come to a standstill, that there are violins playing around you, there is suddenly a breeze and all that while you're looking at that someone special. Don't worry, none of those happened to me, but I was amazed to discover something when I first met this girl, Bandita Arora. Bandita is the name you will be coming across a lot after this.

The junior batch had been admitted and for the first time in history we had an all girls batch. There were six of them. Among them there was this one face I could not resist looking at. No, it wasn't Bandita, it was Maira, her batch-mate who was one year senior to them and just a year junior to me from the same college. I have known her since my undergraduate days and had always wondered what it would be like to go around with her. Fortunately, she was single.

On Fresher's Night I walked up to Maira while all the girls were busy getting drunk at the bar. A few dance moves along with some shots of tequila, and Maira was no less a vegetable leaning on me. The sack was on my hump and I had no idea where to lay it. I could have had her on my bed, but I was turned off somewhere. She could not be taken home in the state that she was in, so post party we decided to head to Bandita's as she was the only one with a 'parent-free' apartment.

Maira puked several times on my rear seat on the way home. The walking tequila bottle was laid in Bandita's room and we sat back on the floor across her bed. It was four in the morning while we sat silently, facing each other. For about twenty minutes neither of us spoke a word. Bandita was probably wondering whether I'd leave and I was wondering if Maira was okay...

"Would you like to have some tea, Sir?" Bandita asked, breaking the silence.

"Sure, should I help?" I replied leaning forward.

"No, that's fine. Sugar, how much?"

"Three spoons."

While Maira seemed to have loosened up, we were relieved talking to each other over the tea.

"So, Bandita, where have you done your BDS from?" I asked slurping my tea.

"Really?" she exclaimed while her big, perfectly outlined eyes gazed in surprise and I looked back at her puzzled. "Seriously, you want to know which college I'm from?"

What had I said?

"I am from the same college where you have done your BDS from," she reverted.

"Really! How is that possible? I mean, how come I never noticed you?"

"May be because you were too busy noticing Varsha Bagdi, Surbhi Rathor, Sonakshi Nathani, Payal Raheja, Siama Rana, Ritu Prihar, and back there, Maira."

That was one hell of a list! I didn't know I had such an impressive record. I blushed and sipped my tea.

"Oh, by the way, there is one tiny help I needed from you," she turned to me.

"Sure, tell me."

"You tell me... did you break up with Varsha Bagdi because she was seeing Choudhary Sir or she walked over you because she found out about your affair with Ritu?"

"Varsha was seeing Choudhary?" I blurted out in surprise.

"You didn't know?"

"I had no idea!"

"Well, so I guess I won."

"What? What do you mean you won?"

"Nothing, we just had a small bet about your rough patch with Varsha. My friends said you guys broke up because you caught her, but I knew that she was much smarter than you were aware of," Bandita said settling on the chair with her legs folded.

I was shocked and amazed. Shocked to learn that I hadn't really been that smart, and amazed to see a girl whom I barely knew knocking me down on my own intellect. She was two years junior to me as well.

I leaned back on the wall folding my legs, "So what else have you girls been up to besides betting on me?" I uttered grinning over my cup.

We chatted all night and it was fun to know stuff about myself that I had been oblivious of until then. I had never spoken to a girl for this long in my entire life. Bandita was no ordinary girl; first of all, she was the first girl who had the guts to have a face-off with me, and secondly, she was the one girl who had me listening to her for three hours straight; and lastly, yeah she was hot!

In no time we started going out. Normally guys and girls see each other over a cup of coffee and use it to stretch the scene further. But in our case we preferred to see each other over mugs of beer. Initially we needed company to drink and we looked for each other, but eventually things turned out the other way. We needed to see each other and we used beer as a reason. However, I wonder why, it was in no way romantic. At times we were hanging out at my place with Hrishabh, and at times at her place with her snotty roommate, who by the way did not drink and hated me for God knows what.

College days were getting tougher as the thesis submission dates neared. I would smoke all night to stay up and work on my subject.

Before the announcement of our preparation leaves, the last conference of the session was to be held at Jaipur. Every year we were to attend at least two conferences to have a respectable assessment sheet. This was the last conference of my PG.

Bandita and I would work all night at my place on the paper presentation and on the final day it all paid off well. By then, Bandita Arora had become Bandy to me. She won the first prize for the presentation and to celebrate the same we skipped the lousy banquet meet where teachers were crowding the bar.

That was party time: we drank, we danced, and we screamed on the roof of 100% Rock Lounge. It was six of us drowned in two bottles of scotch. As the party got over, we moved out swaggering and swinging on each other. Bandita stumbled over her heel and broke it. We sat down to fix it up and chuckled over it for a while. I told everyone to go ahead while we sat there, but decided to stay there for another hour since everyone else had moved back to the hotel already.

Standing on the roof of the lounge, we had a couple of fags and talked absolute gibberish. There was nothing much to talk about but a lot to feel about. I was looking at Bandita and her rawness. Her childlike smile and the tommyrot she would come up with under jingles, her humming the grandma's day's retro songs with every word memorized perfectly; her long thick hair; the beauty of her perfectly finishing the pulpotomy and roughly living life on pizza boxes, cloth junk and beer bottles – I just loved everything about her and wanted to spend every coming moment with her.

"Sir," she snapped at me, "What happened?"

I moved my hand across her waist and pulled her towards myself.

"I love you, Miss Arora," I said holding her beer bottle in the other hand.

✦

It was exam time and things had been more than crazy. Final year PG exams can make even the easiest stag like me wet my collar with sweat. Sometimes the patient did not cooperate, or the external wanted to screw you; in other cases, if it was a lady external, she might want to screw with you! But this time it wasn't the case. My seniors and juniors had been extremely cooperative to make me finally make it.

It was our time for our farewell and Bandita and I were on the floor when once again there was nothing but silence between us. I once again asked her if this meant anything to her but things were as vague to her as they were to me.

Finally the time for me to leave had arrived. I was finally leaving Bangalore forever. All the eight years of striving and insobriety would be gone ju   st like that. Bandita and I stood at the station awaiting the train. Today there was a lot to be said and a lot to be heard. But neither of us had the guts to say anything out loud.

That was the one time I realized that I was not that smart with girls. I might have had the experience of asking them out or to get in their pants, but I had missed learning the real thing – proposing to a girl. I wished there was something that could help me convert my feelings into words, for I was not the guy who could come up with cheesy sentences, wheedle girls, pamper them to win their approval and never take 'no' for an answer and keep trying. My train had come, but not the few words I had wanted.

"So, I guess it's time. I should go," I sighed looking at my luggage and just then Bandita held my palm and gave me a small peck on the cheek and hugged me tight as though she knew that there would never be a second time. I took her in my arms and smelled the lavender in her hair. That was one moment I wish had stood still, the one moment when I could feel just us and nothing around.

I flicked the curls at the back of her ear and whispered, "Marry me."

She looked at me with moist eyes and the signal blew. Once again, words had fallen short. We parted looking at each other till the last sight.

The next morning my life at home began. On the one hand while I was still unemployed and perturbed about starting a whole new life where there was no Hrishabh and me switching the TV remote buttons over a football match along with biryani and beer, no motor bike to wander around the city, no Bandita and her silly talk to listen to, and most importantly, no city in the first place. In a city like Ahmedabad, the understatement 'dry' can truly dry you from the throat to down there. And topping the icky routine were my parents, who wanted me to get married as soon as possible.

Being from a typical Gujarati family, the Patel community-16 gaon, where guys of my age were probably on the verge of getting a vasectomy done after two kids, I was running late already. Besides, keeping in mind my earlier failed affair to which my parents had almost agreed to me eloping with the girl and marrying her before she left me, they feared considering love marriage again would be a risky affair. In their eyes I had no idea about my own well being so should be tied to a well-trained *garba*-dancing and *thepla*-making girl.

The horses were goaded to find me the perfect match and before I could tell them about Bandita, I was already overruled. In sixteen days, I had seen pictures of more than sixteen girls.

Meanwhile I kept convincing Bandita to make up her mind but I had no idea that there was very little time left. My sisters had come down from Canada to celebrate the birth of her new-born child, and they had been planning it along with my birthday which was exactly thirteen days away – the 13th of November.

Before things could get moving between Bandita and me, I was suddenly meeting a girl at the party on my birthday. Relatives filled the house and I could hardly speak to Bandita. Things had moved pretty fast; from liking to loving to willing to marry her. And all the while my parents had been looking for a girl for me. Every time I tried bringing up Bandita's name or telling them why I was not willing to marry anyone at the point, they would just hush me up. Despite the 'broad spectrum' vision that my family had given me up till now, it was all going in vain in the name of marriage.

We had moved to our native place, Ananad, for the function. I was introduced to a girl named Sapna Patel. Sapna too was a doctor and a family friend who I had known through the bio-data charts for around a year now. But no matter what, I was going to reject her.

Sapna had been constantly around me and so were our parents. I tried messaging Bandita and started looking for a corner where I'd get a signal, and the next thing I know my dad was on stage commencing the ceremonies. I tapped my cell when I heard something that knocked my socks off – my engagement with Sapna.

I had nowhere to go, nothing to do and no way to react to it. I couldn't smile, couldn't deny it, nor could I run away. The next morning I woke up as someone's fiancé; someone whom I barely knew and had absolutely no feelings for. I had no balls to turn to Bandita after all this. I kept talking to her like nothing had happened. I knew that I should tell her, but what could I have said? I had no explanation and didn't know how would I have consoled her.

I had talked to my parents again, but it was a fruitless attempt. I made a plan to visit Bangalore and meet Bandita. I did not know how would I be breaking the ice, and I did not know whether or not I should do it this way, but all I knew then was that I needed to see her. I needed to be with her; if not for her, then for myself, but it was important to meet her one last time – if at all it was the last time.

This time she had come to receive me at the station. I had never seen Bandita so enticed about anything. She hugged me as I stepped towards her saying, "Marry me." I hugged her and said, "I missed you."

We spent the next three days together at my place. I narrated the sequence of events to Hrishabh since I needed to vent it out to someone.

On the last day of my stay, Bandita and I were sitting on the roof of my house sipping beer as we always did. I had never seen Bandita happier. She did not wish to leave me even for a minute. We talked the whole night. She plucked the opener ring from the beer can and leaned into my arms.

She took my hands in hers and said, "Parth Patel, will you marry me?" and she put the ring in my ring finger.

I wrapped her in my arms and said, "I love you, Bandita, no matter what. What we have is and will always be very special to me," I said holding my tears back. I had never been so sure about anyone before and the feeling was beautiful. Even the little pain that lay in it was beautiful and I would fall in love again and again with her. While she sat beside me, all of a sudden all the things about lovers that once appeared stupid to me, made sense. I was head over heels in love with this girl and could not let her go just like that from my life. We spent the whole night next to each other having beer.

The next morning I left without letting out even a bit of what was going within me. I still hoped to talk my parents into this. Reaching home I asked them once again if anything made any sense to them.

"I am not ready for marriage and definitely not with this girl," I yelled

"This girl's name is Sapna and she is going to be your wife," my dad retorted.

"Why are you doing this to me? I will never be able to love her and keep her happy. This will ruin both our lives. Will you be happy after that, looking at me unhappy and unstable? What is the rush? Why do you want me to get married right away? I am not prepared."

"You are ageing, son. Another year from now and there won't be any girls left in our community who would want to marry you. Sapna is the perfect girl for you. You will fall in love with her eventually."

"I *am* in love with Bandita. At least meet her once, and talk to her once. I am sure you would…"

"I am sure? You were sure the last time as well. But she never showed up, did she? We can't sit back with your assurance. My decision is final and if you wish to go against me, expect an ad in the newspaper disowning you. Then you will be free to do whatever you want to," my dad said and left. My mother wept as all she wanted me to say was yes.

Ever since I had learned the phrase – decision-making – in my life, I have never really made any. Dad was a Ph.D. in science; he made me opt for science in high school. He wanted me to be a doctor; I completed my BDS. He said I must study further so I completed my MDS too. He asked me to come back to set up my own clinic, and I did just that. In the midst of all this, I never realized that I had forgotten to think for myself. I had no clue how to figure out the strength that lay inside me. Now they wanted me to get married to a girl of their choice, keeping the gun on my future. I guess I had no choice!

The next day I called Hrishabh and asked him to break the news of my engagement to Bandita. I informed him of my wedding date, which was twenty days away. The 14th of December, 2014.

I switched off my cell and deleted my social network accounts. I knew what I was doing was wrong, but I had chickened out. I had no fortitude left to face anyone.

Hrishabh broke the news to Bandita the next day. At first she did not believe him and tried reaching me to find out the truth. I returned none of her calls. I did not know how to answer her. Finally I called her at midnight. She sobbed heartbreakingly as I admitted the truth to her and everything that had happened with me in all these days.

It was tough; tougher for her. I wish I was there to hold her, pamper her, take her in my arms and help her stand again. I conveyed to her how things were out of my hands. Although deep down, we both had not given up hope.

Preparations for the wedding had begun. I still tried to convince my parents. I tried to talk to them about meeting Bandita. I showed them her picture but they doubted if she would marry me. Bandita had not said a word to her family, and how could she have, since things were dicey at my end.

And it so happened, there were not just *my* parents who had a problem with my love life. They say when you really wish for something, obstacles appear from every corner of the world to test your will. I guess the verification of genuineness had just begun at my Lord's office.

The talk with my parents

I had always been one of those guys who would live and die for friends. One such close friend in my junior years of PG was a senior, Sonam. We had bonded really well. Sonam, I and another batch-mate of hers, Shivani ma'am, were thick. We used to sit in their hostel room smoking Jaggu troubles. Jaggu was the Head of Department whom was nicknamed Maa Jagdambe. Jaggu was the title awarded to her in the name of her excellence in dominating other teachers and students in the college and her husband back at home who happened to be her junior.

Sonam was married, but had a troubled married life, Shivani was too swollen to fit into a guy's lap, and I was dealing with my own troubles. That's exactly when destiny had brought the three knocked down draggers together. We had been like each other's back-up. We backed each other when it came to mentioning credits under the thesis, when it came to assistance during the practicals, when it came to arranging a back-up patient for the exam or to arrange a back-up bottle. Sonam and Shivani would study all night, while a day before the exam, I would get all the possible help from them.

Sonam eventually separated from her husband and was on the verge of tying the knot once again. Since it was Parth Patel's life, all kinds of gossip would be doing the rounds in VKDS. Sonam had got the news about Bandita and had also got a report on Bandita. In no time, there was a whole character certificate underlined in her name. Sonam reported to my parents about Bandita.

While on the one hand I made my parents take a look at Bandita's picture, Sonam reached them with her character outline, which didn't sound too good to them by the way. According to her, she was an alcoholic, a Casanova, a loaner, and had done this to many guys before.

Amidst all the nonsense that Sonam made up, there happened to be a picture that boggled everyone. Someone from a fake profile on a social networking site sent a picture of Bandita to my sister through an MMS.

We had no idea who really sent the message. At one point I had my finger pointing at Manas, who was Bandita's ex. She was however a hundred percent sure that he had not done it. On the other hand, it could have been someone from the college, but then no one except Hrishabh from college really knew the whole scene. At the end, our eyes were on Sonam for she was the only one making up stories all the time and who was in touch with my family. But it was no obvious condition. I wondered why Sonam would do that. She had rather been more than a well wisher. The MMS mystery had driven my family to crosswords. Once again, they were deluded to misconceive my choice.

But somewhere there was a little hope tied up to my sister Roopali, who could have balanced the equation. I convinced her to talk to Bandita just once and then decide if what I was doing was correct or not.

The talk with my sister

I had all my hopes pinned on Roopali. Only her words could get my parents to consider meeting Bandita. That night Roopali called up Bandita to understand if my recitations were of any worth.

"It has been just a month and you are saying that you are ready for marriage. Are you really sure, Bandita?" Roopali asked.

"I guess I am. I know we have not known each other too long, but I know one thing for sure that neither of us has been so sure ever before. I understand that the past might make you doubt us, but I can assure you that I will not turn around," replied Bandita.

"I do not doubt your love or my brother's choice, Bandita, but things are on the edge and it is very difficult to even contemplate reversing them," accentuated Roopali.

"All the preparations have been done, celebrations have started, and the wedding has been announced. How we are supposed to talk Sapna out of it? You are a girl; you can understand how difficult it would be for her to overcome this."

"How difficult will it be? They have just been engaged for a few days and barely know each other. How can an engagement of fifteen days compete against a relationship of a year? How is that justice?"

"Bandita, I don't know what you have been told, but I feel that you think this engagement took place just a few days back and all of a sudden, right?"

"What do you mean?" asked Bandy.

"Sapna and Parth have been in touch with each other for a year now," Roopali replied over a long silence. "I don't know what Parth has told you, but the two have known about the families wanting them to get married for a year and have known each other since childhood. Sapna is in love with Parth, which is why she agreed to wait for him for another year. I am amazed how Parth never mentioned this to you."

"I had no idea at all. All I know about this is through Sir. Apparently it was not the entire truth. Thanks for the information and here I was feeling sorry for a guy who I thought was being forced to get married."

"I am sorry that you have been kept in dark all this time. I did not expect this from Parth, but now you know what is holding us back."

"I completely understand, Roopali, and I guess I know what will be holding me back now. The show must go on. I don't know about Parth, but at least Sapna deserves a happy ending," Bandita assured Roopali that she'd step back.

I was once told that nothing good comes out when two ladies talk; I couldn't agree more after this. No, Roopali did not lie about the engagement, but yes, it meant nothing to me!

Sapna's family and mine had been talking about our marriage for almost a year now, but I had never spoken to her. I knew that Sapna liked me and could have married me for the worst, but the engagement was instantaneous. I still wanted Bandita and I never lied to her about anything. May be I was timid at some point about giving details, but then again, the details didn't matter, unless I had known that things would be brought up this way.

Thirty-seven calls. It took me exactly thirty-seven calls to make Bandita understand the same thing. Talking to my parents was out of the question and talking to my sister did not do any good, but there was one person who could still do the job.

The talk with Sapna

The days were passing by swiftly and I couldn't erase everything in a moment, so I decided to go and talk to Sapna about the whole scene. I was sure that anyone would step back knowing that the groom to be was still engaged in his past affair. I assured Bandita that I would be talking Sapna out of this engagement and would come clean about our relationship to her parents. What could possibly feed this wedding further?

Bandita had gathered hope again and made her mind to announce our relationship to her family once I called off this engagement. Another sigh of relief, another hope for the good, another strand of faith in the strength of our relationship; once again I was sure about my choice. This time I was very sure about my choice – even if my dad was not – and I had taken a decision in favour of my opinion about my life.

I started the six-hour drive from Ahmedabad to Vadodara, where Sapna resided. I had to clear the haze between me and Bandita and had to make sure she'd trust me once again. From eight in the evening to two in the morning, every second was like the ticking of a time bomb. I had no clue about what I was going to say to Sapna's parents. How would Sapna hold herself, and how would the situation be accepted in our community? All I had safe in my mind was that I wanted to spend the rest of my life with Bandita. I promised myself that if this ever happened, I would quit smoking forever.

But as it is said 'a good vision but a poor strategy is but a waste'. The journey was over, the talk was done, and the time to head back home had come. On my way back to Ahmedabad, I picked up my pack of Classic Milds and kept my phone aside for the rest of the day after leaving a message for Bandita.

I am sorry, Bandy. I know I don't deserve to ask you to understand but that is all I can do at present. I couldn't talk to Sapna's parents. I did tell Sapna about you but she had no issues about anything. Calling off the engagement is a big step and I couldn't do it by myself. I couldn't gather enough guts to tell you when I was with you, when I was at Sapna's and now when I have my parents mourning in front of me. I know it's my fault. I shouldn't have asked you in the first place. I know if someone deserves a reprimand, it's me, but don't worry because it will be me now and for the life ahead. I can't go against my parents. Sorry. You may not understand now, but you will after a few years.

Sent. And my fate was hitched.

A few days later when Bandita had made peace with my decision, I finally made her the closure call.

"Bandita, how are you?"

"I'm fine. You tell me, when is the big day? I hope I am invited to the wedding," Bandita said in a much lighter tone than I had expected.

"I am very sorry to do this to you, Bandy..."

"Sir, first you do one thing, stop calling me Bandy, and then stop saying sorry. You don't have to be sorry, for you don't deserve to ask for forgiveness. Had you really meant it, you would have stood up to your decision. But you chose the easy way instead. You chose to give up. But, anyway, it must be for the good."

"Please don't punish yourself for this, Bandita. We have to be mature at times. I can't let my parents weep over my wishes. You have no idea how insane things have been at my side."

"No hard feelings, and I don't even wish to know what is going on. And trust me, no hard feelings. And yes, I agree it is for the better, since I would like to marry a person who can speak up at the right time and not just over beer."

I wished her all the best in life and put down the phone hoping that at least she was happy to snub me. I was relieved to see my parents smiling. At least they were happy, I was happy to find out that Sapna was excited to shop for her wedding. At least someone was enjoying the preparations. I was happy to receive wishes from my friends when the wedding was announced. At least some people were looking forward to the big day and at last, I was happy to look at myself in the mirror. Once again, I proved to be a great son.

Outside Bengaluru raiway station

I walked out of the station, haggled with the auto rickshaw driver in goony Kannada and hauled my knapsack from the back of the seat. It seemed like one of those moments when I had been working on my patient on the day of my final practical exams, when in the middle of the treatment, he wanted to leave. I had no way to get him back and no way to make it through without getting him back. The pressure – outside and inside – was high. Today was one such moment again. I had nowhere to go. I just preened around the station in antsy and took a deep breath. *Please forgive me, I am sorry, I am sorry. I know this isn't the best thing to do, but I have no choice. I am sorry – I never wanted to hurt you.*

I remember myself in the trial room putting on the sherwani for my wedding. I kept looking at myself in the mirror that day but couldn't find Parth. It was just Parth's body. I didn't feel myself within.

7th December 2014

I looked at the sherwani again and again and the person behind it didn't seem familiar at all. I was to get married in this very sherwani in seven days, with Sapna, and had never imagined in my life that seven days prior to my wedding, this is what I was to feel. I was not happy. I ran my hands against the texture of the garment, but it wasn't really the cloth, it was the person who was behind it. I fell down against the mirror, breaking into tears – in pain, in repentance, in loss. I had lost the one thing I chose for myself. I wept and wept knowing that I had made a wrong decision that would stay with me for life. I wept because my life was going to change in seven days, and it would no longer have Bandita in it.

Sitting in the balcony of my room, I called up Bandita. I told her that I made a wrong decision and it could still be corrected if she stood by me.

The next day I left for Vadodara for Ishan's wedding. He was a friend from college. The return train from Vadodara to Ahmedabad was to depart at 10.30 a.m. It was 10.25 as I sat on the platform eyeing my bogie. The signal had blown and I stood up. There was another signal and I looked around me at people rushing to the train. It had started moving. The windows passed through my eye – coach by coach.

The train to Ahmedabad had left. I reached for the cell phone in my pocket and turned it off. I heard a second announcement of the arrival of the next train to Bangalore in some time. I was going to run away from my own wedding which was in six days and believe me, I had never been worse.

Have you ever felt the tingles when you look at someone, someone special? The feeling that everything has come to stop, that there are violins playing around you, there is suddenly a breeze and all that while you're looking at that someone special? Yes, this time the spot lights were really there and all that very much happened to me when I finally saw Bandita. Trust me, it was all worth it!

I hugged her tight and kissed her long on the forehead. Her arms felt the safest place where I could be and I wished that not even a foe must ever go through the situation that I was in.

She made me some Maggi and we sat on her terrace sipping beer all night.

"So, you finally made it," she said laying her head on my shoulder.

"Still can't believe it. Five days to go for the big day."

"The longest five days of our lives."

"I will get back and apologise after that. They can punish me... I'm ready to face anything."

"*We* are; we are ready to face anything!" Bandita took my hand in hers and said.

The engagement was called off soon after. Sapna's parents were racked, but there was little they could do. My parents did not react the way we expected, and were rather penitent about forcing me to get married. Dad however took some time to get normal.

Bandita avowed her family about our relationship and everything was taken pretty well. My parents even permitted me to study ahead and assured me they were in no rush to get me married. A year of courtship and false runs had finally brought us together.

It was on the night of our *sangeet* that I was talking to my Absolut Vodka on the dressing table, recalling all the events that had finally got us to that moment. Two pegs later, it felt wonderful that I was finally marrying the love of my life. The rings had been exchanged and the party had begun.

After the sangeet, there was a bachelor's night. It was the last night for the groom-to-be to realize that the end of his bachelor life had finally arrived. But before that, there is always some Absolut. I just kept reminding myself of all the pain I had undergone and it was all for the best, the guys told me. But what the guys couldn't do, alcohol did.

Pegs after pegs, pegs after pegs we drank as if that was the last time ever. After all that was the last night of my singlehood.

I woke up the next afternoon, groggy as hell. Gujaratis on one side and Punjabis on the other, dressed in their best, waiting to bless the bride and groom-to-be. But they didn't seem to be too happy. I turn to Bandita, for at least she was happy.

There comes in a nurse to check my pulse. *A nurse!*

It is a hospital and I am the patient.

"Had a little too much last night? Could not make it to your own wedding today. So is there any plan to settle down, Sir?" Bandita laughed out loud.

Apology! Sex Pays

@

There was a black board outside my house that read: Diwakar Sharma, B.A., L.L.B. in white letters. The funny thing is my life completely justified that board; it was black and white.

I never said that I wanted to be a lawyer, believe me, never! But it was something that happened to me – just like my marriage. I never really said that I wished to get married, not even with the girl my parents chose for me, but it happened and it happened pretty early. After completing my BA from a nearby college, my father asked me to join his business. Not some steel pipe manufacturing industry, for we owned a hardware shop in Gadarwada, a small town in Madhya Pradesh, about three hours from Jabalpur. I thought sitting in the shop meant playing video games on my cell phone while selling screw drivers. But that did not work out too well so I decided to continue my studies. I moved back to where I had started my studies: Jabalpur. I did not plan the next step though. After a few days of vagabond trials at the tea stall near the station, I met a friend, who was friends with me for three days. He was a student of MA and stayed in the college hostel. The hostel looked good and seemed decent at just four hundred bucks a month. That sounded like a pretty good deal as I planned ahead. The only condition was that the hostel only entertained college students. So, the very next thing was to get enrolled for MA in the same college.

All day instead of going for classes, we would sit at the tea stall and drag *bidis* with tea. I was the stag of my area and they called me Debu Bhaiya. The first year results were out and I predictably didn't get through; and this continued for another two years. My father ordered me to make reservations in the next train to Gadarwada and get back to joining the shop. Going back to Gadarwada would mean the party would be over. In a year they'd hitch me with a girl and the year next to that a baby would arrive. Debu Bhaiya seemed to be fading away and so did the endless fags. So I planned to enrol myself in the university law college for the LLB course. What took others three years, took me five to become a lawyer.

As soon as my graduation was complete, I started interning under a lawyer when one day my parents called me home in the name of a huge Satyanarayan *katha* that they had organized for our well-being. Under the silhouette of Lord Satyanarayan, they introduced me to a girl who had come to see me with her family. Before I could ogle at her from across the *kaju barfi, gujiya, mathri* and *kachori* on the centre table, we were asked to get into a corner and have a conversation. Within five minutes of knowing each other, we were announced engaged.

I guess that is how it happens in most of our Indian families. Education to please relatives, marriage to please more unpleased relatives, and then kids to please relatives who have suffered all the other pleasures of life.

I have been married for three years today, managing a taxi business in partnership with a friend back in my home town.

The courts didn't like me much. The good news so far was that there were no kids, yet.

Everything else was too insignificant in my life to be called news. My wife has put on over fifteen kilos in these three years and like the monotonous okra-*dal*-rice at dinner, the sex in the dessert didn't taste too sweet.

While those friends of mine who were still practicing in the lower court, found enough chances in the bar room to flirt with the lady advocates – the bar room in the court where the lawyers gathered in the afternoon, however, only for tea and not drinks. If that was not enough, few mavericks were even making out with the interns working under them. But in my case, there happened to be no new faces and no new figures.

Pushpa – the lady running the sandwich corner near my taxi stand is a figure eight and has been divorced from his husband. She has a daughter but I appreciate the way she manages to look no less glamorous than Malaika Arora Khan at this age. The potatoes in her sandwiches are pretty soft. I have been a regular customer there, but sandwiching more than the potatoes doesn't seem to be a good option in a small town. Gadarwada is the size of a mall with fewer people in it. Everyone here knows everyone. Any awry move may end in a lifetime of banishment from the society.

The past three years were therefore all work and no play. Not that bad though as I had saved a lot for myself. Enough to pay back the three years' debt for my hardships. Accounting the three years of profit that we had made through adding more taxis, I planned to invest in having some fun with four of my friends. We planned a trip to Thailand.

Being Asia's biggest and the only legal sex market, the trip to Thailand was to be masqueraded in the name of a business trip to

Delhi. Our bags were packed and our wives were hoodwinked. The flight was off to Bangkok.

Someone had rightly named the city '*Bang cock*'. While coining the name, probably its predators had been practically implying the same.

We had booked a three-day stay in the city. The first night and day were spent exploring the city and its culture on a tuk-tuk. We shopped a little in the day time and partied at night.

My bag was half-filled with condoms and the rest with a few aphrodisiacs – pine nuts, figs, chocolates, whipped cream, cherries and half a dozen of other remedies that I had lately discovered on the internet for a brilliant climax. Other than Thai food, there was another thing that the country is famous for – their Thai massage. Now, here is a fun fact about this massage. It did not really deal with curing your ailments or pulling out adipose from your body through ancient oil remedies, and yet was the most relieving rub one could ask for. It eased down the area of highest tension. But I was saving for the big day – or night!

On the second night, we went to Nana Street which was the footfall of happiness. On the one hand we had Ganga-Jamuna in Nagpur, Kamathipura in Mumbai, Sonagachi in Kolkata and GB road in Delhi with robust over-aged ladies in their sagging old skins and chewing the same old paan to lure customers; on the other there was Nana Street, catering to any man's fantasies. Even one with no hankers left may develop an appetite for the bonhomie once he steps on Nana Street.

The street emblazoned itself with night lights and ladies. The Korean, Thai and Vietnamese pranced on the street, busting out at limousines and philanderers. They would strut around lonely men to see if they were interested in getting some action.

Alongside the streets were small *sheesha* corners, where girls of Russian and Indian origin would lure customers. Unlike the mini-eyed, the girls at the Sheesha corner had their own way of reaching clients. They would take a few drags with the guy and few minutes later, they would ask them if they would like to buy them a drink. A steady and aristocrat move over a few drinks and cheesy chatter was a way to discover what lay within the pants!

The market was huge. It had options from street shopping to huge branded showrooms displaying real girls as mannequins!

I had picked one from the cabin for myself. She was voluptuous. She was mini-eyed and wore an orange dress. Her tush was larger than mine and that justified spending my money.

I bought her a drink and we barely talked before she took me to the hotel. She showed her card and took me to the room on the second floor. Her name on the card was Aiwin, and the sock was left on the door knob. My bucket list was not a long one, but the one wish that would be the first to be crossed off was here.

We relaxed over a few drinks. She asked me if this was my first time over paid sex. I told her I had been doing this since the time I attained puberty but this time I wished to experience the Thai massage.

We were two pegs down. She took off her heels and rubbed her left foot over the calf of her right one. I asked her if she wanted to drink more, and we were soon sipping out third peg.

"So, you are from Thailand?" I enquired

"Aye, you can say so. What have you tried here so far?" she asked me.

"Nothing much, let's see... casinos, wailing over the shopping boats and just a little bit."

"So, you haven't yet tried the sandwich?"

"What sandwich?" I quirked to her even though I had not much interest in eating sandwiches at Bangkok after coming all the way from India; especially when they were available all the time at Pushpa's.

"Oh! So you haven't. Trust me, you'll love it. If you want I can arrange something for you tomorrow."

"Well, are you asking me to eat sandwiches instead of Chinese food in China? Lady, India has a large number of sandwich corners. Tell me something in Chinese, may be that would interest me."

"Okay, first of all – Thailand is not in China, and second of all, you will not find a sandwich like the one I am talking about anywhere but here."

Then she explained what the sandwich was. I was to be the potato in between two ladies, beneath and above me, only that the potatoes would be a lot harder in this one. The thought of a threesome made me drool already and sounded a lot better than those at Pushpa's.

I was ravenous after her explanation. The only issue was that I did not have a lot of money. I asked Aiwin if she could give me a discount and she said she would think about it. Later she locked me in a condition that she would only seal a good deal if I chose her as one of the slices of bread.

She finished her last peg and threw me back on the couch. Leaning forward on my chest, she began to kiss me. I titillated my hands on her waist and pulled her close. Her lips were all over my neck and slowly tickled on my ears, when she bit me on the pinna. Eventually my hands were fondling her softly, when she threw off her dress and stood up. She unhooked her inner wear and slipped it off and settled herself on my lad while she crushed her dress through her loins.

I hustled to wear protection.

"How do you like it?" she whispered in my ears.

"Show me what you have," I responded throwing myself back on the pillow as I closed my eyes.

The next thing that my eyes opened to was something my genitals would never ever forgive me for.

Aiwin pulled off her lingerie and reached to me while my eyes were still shut and before my hand could reach her tush, what I got wasn't quite familiar to me. My hands have never touched anything like that before; I tickled my fingers around but no, nothing close to what I have ever felt before. I wanted to pry over what felt so unexpected down there and whoa! This iPod was a radio with an antenna.

The product was different inside. Yeah! Aiwin was not a girl. She was a she but only with a male organ: a Shemale.

She was kissing me all over my face when I pushed her off.

"What is the matter with you?" she exclaimed.

"What is the matter with *you*? Who the hell are you? You... you aren't that... but that..." I spluttered.

"Oh, come on! You can't back off now. We are so doing it!"

"Are you crazy? I can't do it with you. Leave right now."

"Hell! I am not going anywhere without my payment."

"What payment are you talking about? We didn't do anything. Nothing happened. What will I pay you for?" I yelled at the top of my voice.

"I am still in the room; you can do me right away. I will get my pay and will leave. Simple."

"Just get the hell out of here, and I won't be paying for any of this. Out of my room. Now!"

"No... no... no, Mister. I am not leaving without my pay. Either you do me or I will have to do it my way."

"What? What will you do? Listen, Miss... Mister... it's a mistake, okay? I cannot pay you for something that I have never done," I swallowed my frenzy and turned her towards the door.

"You know that you haven't done anything, but how will you prove it outside?"

"What do you mean?" And before I was through figuring out her words, I was given the worst jerk off that I have ever had. She knocked me without an orgasm and the funny thing was that I was the one left screaming.

She handed me my condom, "This is my proof that you did it. Now, give me my money or I will take it down at the reception and would file a complaint against you exploiting me," she grinned at the sample.

Disgusted at my fate, I handed her the money and showed her the door.

It was the worst thing that could happen to someone in Thailand. I lost my money and was a shameful blot on my character. I could strike it off my bucket list but I had returned a virgin even after getting a quick massage by a doll with balls. Much better are the low maintenance red light areas in our land. At least you know who is who, and you know it before making a choice.

I was back in my own land, to my very own wife, and looking forward to our same old sandwiches at Pushpa's with soft potatoes in between. Maybe destiny had gone for a pee when God asked her to shower her blessings on me.

Papier Blanc
(The Blank Paper)

©

16th June 2004
Delhi

It was around 11'o clock in the morning on a Wednesday at Cafe Coffee Day. I still remember those confused eyes searching for a French word in an English-French dictionary, sipping her cafe frappe and slurping on the straw to suck out the last drop. I had known Kiara for about one-and-a-half years now, but it seemed we had known each other forever. Only six months back she had moved in to my apartment from her hostel.

"Bonjour, Madam Suzane," Kiara closed her laptop and picked up her study material and left me with my coffee and her morning greetings.

"You are leaving already?" I muttered seeing her leave.

"Yes, I have my class in ten minutes and as always I am already late."

Kiara was learning French those days. She has been quite a writer at the same time and wished to study French literature and eventually write books in French. Long story short, I had no idea of what she spoke most of the time except the one word that she taught me – *'hurluburlu'* which meant eccentric.

Pushing the door that clearly said 'pull', she left.

January 2013
(From Suzane's diary)
Vidyasagar Institute of Mental Health and Neurosciences, Delhi

I have never liked hospitals. The stark whiteness all around, the smell of blood and spirit and the glow from the OT lights that were switched on were in itself enough to make you realize that things were not going so well.

I was asked to wait outside in the visitors' room by the time the patient was prepared to meet me. Sanatoriums and mental health care hospitals have their own rules about allowing patients to meet their concerned visitors. An advance request, a formal cross check of the related visitor and the condition of the patient is considered before any outsider is permitted in the room.

After twenty minutes of waiting, I was let inside the room. It was an empty room with white walls. There was bedding on the left corner that had clearly been hurled aside and I could see the same confused eyes in front of me, but this time they were trying to search for existence beyond a few French words.

"Kiara," I called. "Hi, do you remember me? It's me, Suzane."

Kiara's eyes stood gazing at me longing for a clue somewhere.

Few years back

It was not a Saturday night. Kiara and I were sitting in our balcony with a bottle of rum and two glasses waiting to get filled. We loved talking, and talking over drinks was added pleasure. We discussed the whole world over 2 pegs, right down to the tiniest details. And to the remorse of the world we did not just talk about guys, in fact hardly about them. Our bone of contention varied from silly G-talks to workplace issues, from spirituality to literature, politics and art to anything we observed in and around us. Our careers were definitely one of them.

That day we were discussing a guy. I had recently met a guy in a cafe. He had approached me in the cafe and we spoke casually. I do not even remember about what but what I do remember is that he was cute, smart, intelligent, and some kind of writer.

"Writer. That reminds me that he was writing a book on body language and he had been observing me for some time as I sat alone. A minute later, he walked up to me and shared with me his theory of judging someone by one's body language." I narrated the incident to Kiara and it made her more and more interested in him. The night passed by under the moonlight. It was cold that night, but not unpleasantly so. And so our chatter continued long through the night.

The next morning, like any other, we were getting ready for college. We both were studying at Jamia Millia University. I was in my second year of communication management and Kiara was discovering herself through Master's in French literature. She had published articles in French journals a couple of times, besides her two published novels in English which, however, didn't do quite well in the market.

Life was going on smoothly for me, but not so much for Kiara, and the sad part is that I had no knowledge of that. There still lies a mist over what happened to her and how it led to the estrangement between us.

Kiara belonged to a Malayalam Christian family, but since her dad was posted in railways, she had resided across the country well enough to forget that she should be speaking Malayalam as well besides French. Although she did remember a few words from her native language, it was hardly sufficient to form a coherent sentence.

Her father had killed himself when she was in junior college. Kiara returned home with her intermediate results when she found her mother sitting beside her dad who lay on the floor, still. She had topped that year but she never got a chance to celebrate her win. Her dad had had a leg amputation as a result of long standing diabetes and that drowned him into depression. Later he learned that he was suffering from cancer and chose to kill himself before the cancer could kill him.

To Kiara, her father's death was never acceptable. She thought that he had been too weak to let his life go.

In the first year of her graduation, she got her first French poem published and won many awards thereafter for her writing. But, she was not satisfied. She wished to write a book and couldn't begin. There were too many thoughts in her mind.

"*Excuse moi*, Ma'am." One of the students at the university walked up to Kiara.

"*Oui*," Kiara turned to him.

"*Sil vous plait aide moi avec ces unit*," he said asking for help in a chapter.

While helping him, Kiara was lauded for her French compositions that got published in the journals earlier that year.

"*Il es un timbre*. Tembre means a little stupid..." Kiara explained.

"Great, Ma'am. I love the way you explain. You must teach French in future.

"Yes, may be in the distant future. As of now, I wish to concentrate on my writing," Kiara chuckled. "What is your name by the way?"

"Arjun; B.A. final year."

"It was nice meeting you, Arjun."

Later in the evening, while we were at our farewell party, Kiara narrated the incident to me, though she forgot to recall the student's name. Meanwhile, one of the staff members walked in and offered Kiara a one-year internship in France for the teaching programme.

This was huge. Kiara was the first one to be offered an internship without any application. We raised a toast to it. She was very happy that day and even though she had no plans of getting into teaching, she had always wished to visit France and live there for a while.

I had never seen Kiara this happy before, for there had always been some discontentment within her as she believed that she never got what she deserved. She worked her blood and sweat, but could not reach anywhere, so it was no wonder she was a writer. I believe there is a species on this earth that could never be happy enough – writers.

Kiara was dating Aakash those days. Aakash was an architect by profession and passion and was a guy few women would covet. But, there it was; Kiara was just not any woman. Aakash and Kiara knew each other through me and in no time were best friends. It had just been a few months when Aakash asked her out. And by the time they were back home, the guy had made up his mind to marry her. Kiara, however, could not yet see it going anywhere. There was no connection according to her. She considered him a friend and just to satiate his feelings, she had herself into the flow. There was nothing they would not talk about or share. Kiara did not have to put any extra effort to go out with him, but somewhere Aakash wasn't too oblivious of that, and it did make him very insecure.

Kiara had no plans of settling down at that time. In fact, she would say that she had no plans of getting settled at all.

I personally feel that to settle down with someone, one needs to settle down with oneself. Accept where one is and what one has.

There is no end to expectations and nothing like a last desire; it's time that falls short for our endless desires.

Looking at Kiara, at some point she may convince you that she was in love with Aakash but the very next moment after he left, we had a different Kiara – a Kiara who was a fierce, rational, objective woman to whom Aakash was just someone she would discuss her tommyrot ideas with. The only thing in her life that she loved more than herself was her work; her writing, her language, her thesaurus and those green stick notes with French word meanings hanging over her bed. And that was the only thing that kept her from settling down with Aakash.

Writers aren't just any people. They are insane, eccentric, unsettled and seek the most unusual things. But, then again, it's this same nature that pushes them to compose such profound poetry. For most people like us who spend most of our time thinking practically and logically about jobs, kids, houses and mortgages, we are never compelled to contemplate the eternal continuity of life as reflects in the simplest things of life.

Exams were around the corner and both of us were immersed in work. Kiara was also working on a play she was to perform in at the college called La vie en Rose. The famous drama was based on the unusually tragic love life of the singer Edith Piaf. Piaf lost her love in a plane crash and thereafter suffered through the grief of losing her amour for life. Kiara was in the lead and practiced the dialogues all day long. She herself had worked on the script sitting in one corner of the room, plucking the ends of her hair, one of the weirdest habits I have ever observed. As she delved into her own thoughts, fingers would unintentionally get into her hair. She moved them gently from root to ends and plucked its ends unconsciously.

"*C'est lui pour moi, moi pour lui dans la vie Il me l'a dit, l'a juré pour la vie* (It's him for me, me for him in life. He said that to me, swore to me forever)," Kiara recited aloud on the stage,

"*Quand il me prend dans ses brasIl me parle tout bas Je vois la vie en rose* (When he takes me in his arms, he speaks to me in a very low voice, I see life as if it were rose-colored-glasses)," she added.

Edith Piaf could not overcome the dolour over the demise of his lover. She developed amnesia and as she aged, it only got worse. I watched Kiara at the podium and it was as though she was Edith herself. While she stood up there in the black-collared English dress with her hair rolled in, she proved that she was not just a fine writer, but also a brilliant stage actress.

Exams were up and so was Kiara's time in Delhi. Kiara moved to France for her internship.

I talked to her once in a while. When things were unfamiliar and novel to both of us, we chatted almost daily. She explained all that came her way; the beaches where people lay all day long to tan themselves, how every order at the cafe brought her just a spoonful of coffee and that too black if not made clear; how most people could not communicate with her in English, how casually people smoked and smooched in public, more casually than we sip tea, and loads of other stuff.

People there were extraordinarily keen about their style; and why not, after all, it was France. They did not consider any other fashion better than theirs. Kiara had been across the country, including Paris, the city of love. I could not forget that night when she called me instead of our regular internet video calling. She told me that she had found someone named Derik Thomas. He was someone she had only pondered about in a dream and someone whom she could live the rest of her life with. I had never heard her so happy. She was happy: happy like an American.

Derik was an editor of French journals. They met at a French writers' convention and happened to talk over few glasses of wine. Kiara had known him for some years through his work in the journals and always looked up to him. Derik asked her to dance with him at the symposium and they fended off the night as fellow conventioneers.

Few days later, while learning about the types of cheese in a French bakery, Kiara beckoned to an English man questioning the baker on the taste of cheese. Walking few steps towards the familiar voice, he turned out to be Derik.

"*Bonjour Moiseur* (Hi sir)," Kiara leaned forward to catch his attention.

"*Bonjour. Ah! Bonjour Madmosel* (Hi. Ah! Hi Miss)." Derik turned to her. "*Commo ca va?* (How are you?)," he asked her, enthralled by her appearance.

"*Ca va bein. Et vous et que-est-que cest avec le fromage?* (I am fine, what about you and what is it with the cheese?)," Kiara enquired smiling at him.

Derik held his gaze for a few seconds, as if he was quite taken away by her beguiling smile, her pony tail, her red-shining lipstick and the beige frock with the English floral print on it that she wore.

"*Se revile pas mon palais* (Does not wake my palate)," he said softly eyeing Kiara.

They took a walk to the nearby cafe and talked for hours over six cups of coffee with very little milk in it. That was the first of many more coffee dates and they started seeing each other frequently. They had similar interests, they belonged to a similar field and understood each other well; it was an instant French connection. More than that, Kiara was inspired by his philosophy of life. She had never spoken to anyone like him in India. She eventually took to his ideas and beliefs, and within no time she was talking like him. The same Kiara who had no interest in music, rather hated people humming around her, had developed a knack for it. She started discovering a variety of music – attending jazz concerts in her city and tried learning the guitar as well. The guy was quite a singer and Kiara was so flattered with his voice that she would listen to him all day long rather than tune into the radio in her room.

The more she was enraptured by Derik's voice, the more she she became indifferent to Aakash's. They hardly talked on the phone and Kiara never returned his messages. Eventually Aakash and I drifted away from her life. I hardly heard from her. I too had started seeing someone, which left me very little time to think about her.

The same year, in the month of August, Kiara got her fiction story published in one of the ten best short stories collection chosen by the Strasbourg University. She was also awarded for her work in French literature by them.

It was a big day, Kiara was called up on stage. Dressed in the red gown, she took to the dance floor with Derik. They had a lot of wine that night. Walking back home, while Kiara carried her stilettos in one hand and fidgeted from pole to pole on the street, Derik watched her as he walked calmly by her side. In the middle of a sudden shower, he caught her hand and pulled her towards him. He kissed her holding her face in his palms, very much the French way. They made love that night.

It was the best time of Kiara's life. I heard from her for the last time when she told me that Derik had left her a love note on the bed with a necklace on it. It was then that she told me that she could picture her future with Derek and nobody else.

After winter comes spring, and Kiara's life had been sailing smooth. But who knew that the spring wouldn't last much longer. Kiara's wading success had struck Derik. Out of the blue, Derik stopped responding to Kiara's calls and messages. Kiara visited him to confront him, but he didn't owe her any answers. He had never talked of commitment. Kiara had heard from the linguistic wing staff about his philandering side, but nothing seemed more important to her than being with Derik at that time. She never blamed him.

Derik kept making excuses and seeing other girls at the same time. Kiara also heard how he picked a new intern from a different country and moved on after one month of dating. There was no sign that would have made the picture clear to Kiara then. Derik was a chronic drinker. He visited nightclubs every night and drank till he was barely able to get back home. He was never found at his place and had blocked Kiara from his contacts.

Kiara tried and tried, but he had made his final words with her and called off the affair. He, although never made it clear to her the reason behind the split. Few weeks later, she was shocked when Derik resigned from his job and left the city. Kiara was torn. She had lost all mediums of contact with Derik. No one knew where he was. He did not have enough friends in the college, only enough bitches, but even they did not have any idea about his whereabouts. A month later, she heard he was in Paris staying in a hotel for a few weeks. Kiara took a train to Paris. She picked a bunch of lilies to see her beloved in the Hotel Le Louvre, where Derik was staying and requested to meet him at the reception. But Derik refused to see her. Kiara waited for three days in the hotel lobby to catch a glimpse of him, but he never showed up. He kept himself locked in the room, drinking and writing. Three days after sitting on the couch of the hotel with a bunch of dry lilies and wet eyes, when Kiara woke up the next morning, Derik had checked out from the hotel.

Once again she lost all ways to contact him. Completing six months of her internship, Kiara returned to India with reference letters, recommendations, published articles and an appreciation trophy for her writing. But despite all the achievements on her file, it seemed that she had left her soul back in Paris.

Kiara moved to Nainital to stay with her aunt. She never contacted me or Aakash after returning. The whole affair with Derik had ripped her apart. She wanted nothing to do with any relationships in her life. Her focus was only on her writing and her search for solitude shelled her into the past.

Her love for Derik and the anguish of losing him increased every day. She wrote seven poems in that period which described her desolate state of mind and her memories from France. She barely talked to anyone or even moved out of her room. Her meals were served on her desk and the little that she spoke was limited to her complaints about the coffee; it did not taste the same as it did in the French cafes.

Kiara stayed up long at night wondering about the phases of her life as she plucked her hair sitting under the corner lamp in her room.

One morning her aunt noticed the lights of her room still on and moved in to put off the switch. As she muttered to Kiara to get some rest, she turned back to her and screamed aloud in fright.

She found Kiara sitting in the corner of her room with a bunch of her hair fallen around her. She had pulled out strands of her hair the entire night. There were bald patches across her scalp.

"Can't think of anything," she said, "I can't write anymore. What will I write? Can't think of anything," she kept repeating the whole day.

The very day she was taken to the hospital. Kiara was under depression the doctors said and advised her to undergo therapy. She took counselling sessions with a psychologist.

In line with her sessions, she enrolled herself in a writing class taught by a chain smoker named Allyn D'rose, who used his own shoe as an ashtray. Kiara enjoyed learning through him. But during the period of her learning, she complained to her psychologist of having trouble remembering things. She tried memorising Allyn's sayings and tips, but by the time she turned home, all she was left with were the words from her vocabulary list. Her word power seemed to be the only loyal thing in her life.

Often when she failed to stand strong on her psychologist's prescriptions and practices, she would blame it on her forgetfulness, even when she actually remembered.

Allyn's personality had a great influence on Kiara. A person with the knowledge of five languages – English, French, Italian, Spanish and German – he helped Kiara revive an inspiration in her life and this encouraged her back into writing.

After completing her counselling sessions, Kiara moved back to Delhi.

I still remember seeing her after almost one-and-a-half years, and finding it difficult to relate to the Kiara whom I had known earlier. She was extremely lean with short hair and had dark circles around her eyes. The glitter in her eyes was lost and so was the animated tone in her voice. She told me about everything that had happened and that she was ready to start afresh.

Kiara accepted an offer in the university as an associate professor and tried focusing on her career. Aakash was back in her life and was more than happy to see her back. He supported her through the distress and pressures of work life.

One day while taking a lecture in the undergraduate class, while Kiara talked about French culture to her students, she felt like being carried away by her past. Breaking her reminiscence, she went back to the chapter, but could not recognise any of it. She read through the chapter from the beginning but could not recall her lessons. She went through the words and recited their literal meanings in each sentence.

She headed back home and realized that she was gradually losing her memory. With every day, Kiara memorised every lesson as hard as possible and made notes of them in case of a blank out in front of her students. Kiara was managing her lectures through literal translations, for no matter how hard she tried, she missed out on grammar, concepts, facts and references that left nothing to base her teachings on. Her lectures eventually ended up being literal translations and no significant learning from the lessons.

Aakash helped Kiara to practice memory tricks. It was never any easier, but Aakash's love helped her to gather her fallen pieces back. She told Aakash about Derik and he never made hoopla of what had occurred in the past. After a long time, I could see she was happy again. She was turning more optimistic towards her life as she dated Aakash. It looked like the clock had turned around and the three of us were back to the old days.

It was the 24th of December. Kiara's birthday. We along with our friends had gathered at our place to celebrate. That night we all laughed and drank to old times and a few beers down, Aakash proposed Kiara to marry him. Kiara leaned into his arms and kissed him. She pulled his shirt off and they spent the night in each other's arms.

Kiara was not sure about getting married, but was considering it. She liked Aakash but not more than a friend yet. In her mind, she still longed for Derik, though she never said it. She never spoke about Akash the same way she did about Derik. And in order to overcome her urge to get Derik back in her life, she was holding Aakash on the rebound.

Kiara kept him hanging, but Aakash was willing to take his chances.

Kiara's workload increased as her memory got blurry with time. Her doctor advised her to rest and give up learning for some time. Her brain needed rest. But in contravene to that, in order to overcome the stress she received while trying to recollect things, she stressed herself even more to work towards it. She sat down with a pen and paper jotting down notes which she eventually had to do for even her A1 lessons. Kiara was going through severe amnesia.

She had turned herself into a maniac and suddenly nothing was more important to her than her notes. The walls of her room were covered with sticky notes.

She had no time to talk to anyone, no time for her relationship with Aakash and not enough to even look around her. After a point I had forgotten her existence. She would lock herself in the room and switch off her phone, making notes and memorising her lessons. The more she mugged up, the more she had to strain her mind.

Aakash was done trying. Kiara slept with him but woke up feeling nothing for him. She was simply looking for a shoulder to support while she still craved for Derik in her life. Aakash was getting hurt in the process. It was time for him to walk out on Kiara. Their relationship did not seem going anywhere. He asked her to turn to him only if she makes up her mind to marry him.

Kiara was once again alone. She was in no place to make up her mind to settle down with a guy she didn't love but very much needed in her life. Every time she made an effort to crawl up with crippled limbs, she was thrown back.

A month later she discovered that Aakash was seeing some other girl. This was more than she could handle. Kiara gave up all hope. She tried her hand at writing again as words remained loyal in her life. They never left her mind, besides Derik's name. She had unknowingly developed a pattern where stress would rarely leave her. First it was her father's death, then Derik's disappearance from her life, and then the one person she would always cling on to, her best friend Aakash, had pushed her away from his life.

One month ago

One morning she woke up and took the red gown from her closet. She got dressed like she had done the night with Derik and watched herself in the mirror. I woke up listening to her voice. Walking up to her room I saw the lady in the beautiful dress dancing to the lyrics of *'Rien-rien-rien, la vie ne vaut rien...'* (nothing-nothing-nothing, life wants nothing). It looked like the mushroom cloud had parted way from her. She sang, danced and made me dance with her.

"Nothing; I want nothing in my life. Nothing at all. I am happy as hell," Kiara exclaimed.

"Nothing. Yes nothing. Life is great like this," I joined in.

"*Il est entré dans mon coeur une part de bonheur dont je connais la cause* (He has entered into my heart a piece of happiness, the cause of which I recognize)," she said her lines from *Le Vie en Rose*.

"Just Derick," Kiara said smiling at me and then broke into tears, "but he never shows up, Suzane. Marcel never showed up to Piaf. They all do this. They show you love and then disappear. It's very difficult to live now. It hurts so much," she mourned holding my arm...

January 2013
(From Suzane's diary)
As I sat next to Kiara at the back seat of the car.

I didn't know what to say then and I don't know what to say now. Kiara possibly knew whom she was with, but her mind is a blank paper now; no memories, no relevance, no incidents to share. No Kiara.

One month ago

...she mourned holding my arm when I noticed the scars on her wrist. Some were fresh; some were dry. There were not just one or two, but six of those. I asked Kiara about it and she revealed that she had made attempts to kill herself. She said that she just wanted to see if she had enough courage to die.

"It is tough living now," she said.

Kiara was taken to Vidyasagar Institute of Mental Health and Neurosciences, Delhi. She was given shock treatments and she was kept there for a month. Kiara was just a body by the end of that month. I brought her with me to get her soul back.

4th February 2013
Present day

It was a Sunday morning and no one had ever wished to wake up to the smell of fumes on a Sunday morning. I woke up at the knock on the door. The cold Sunday morning made it difficult for me to pull off my rug. I was dozy from the previous night's drinking session as well.

There was a sudden commotion from outside that made me get up with a start.

I reached my bedroom door but it seemed to be locked. I tried opening it and then noticed that it was blocked from beneath with wet towels. I pulled the door open with all my might and there was smoke around me. The whole room was smoking out. Our fire alarm was on and there were firemen. I ran towards the exit suspecting fire. The firemen ran in dousing the flames.

16th January 2013
(From Suzane's diary)

Kiara was home again. She could not recognize me, nor herself. She didn't speak at first. I had cleared her room of her sticky notes and it was back to what it used to look like before she had left for France. She never asked me anything about herself or about me, but just stared blank and kept mum. A week long silence finally broke when she subconsciously uttered:

"*Quand il me prend dans ses bras il me parle tout bas Je vois la vie en rose.*" (When he takes me in his arms, he speaks to me in a very low voice, I see life as if it were rose-coloured-glasses.)

"I still remember some of it," Kiara smiled at me and saw me off to work thereafter. I was happy she was back, and back smiling. She showed improvement with time. We watched movies, snacked together and selected the perfect dress for my blind dates.

Just a night before the accident, we were laughing at old memories over rum in the balcony, just as we used to before. I was very happy to finally find Kiara relieved of her past. We did not scratch any dried wounds. Kiara was getting back to the present and was ready to relive life. We planned her to pick a new profession that had nothing to do with French or English, like being a dancer – she could have worked on her moves, or selling her French notes which would make one thick textbook, or be a wine taster, provided she did not drink the whole bottle of wine in order to get the taste of it.

The fire was attributed to a burst oven.

I moved into my room and Kiara did to hers. She pushed her door till she could see me getting in and then went to grab another glass of rum in the balcony. She took her first few quaffs and lay back on the easy chair looking at the stars above. She tapped on my bedroom window from outside as she finished her glass. Then she wiped the last drop off her lips and her tears off her eyes.

I walked up to the kitchen to look at the burst oven but could not believe what I saw. I was taken aback by the sight in front of me and time seemed to have stopped for a moment.

She had moved towards the kitchen weeping quietly as she covered the short distance. She locked the kitchen door and sealed its door, knelt in front of the oven and turned on the gas knob.

I was standing still in front of her burnt body with her head inside the oven. She died of carbon monoxide poisoning and made sure to seal my room with tape and wet towels to protect me from the smoke.

Ernest Hemingway said, "If you are lucky enough to have lived in Paris as a young man, then wherever you go for the rest of your life, it stays with you – for Paris is a moveable feast." Kiara lived with her feast till the very end.

I would live the first life that I would be offered again.
I would love the first job I would learn doing again.
I would marry the first guy who'd ask me to dance with him again.
I would want all of it and would not cry again.
I have nothing to live with now, for nothing has stayed for too long.
I held the blank paper of my life and words may never show up again.

—Kiara Davidson

When All That
Mattered Was A Gun

©

It was the days when we resided in the college hostel. I was in my final year of engineering then and there was a lot of pressure as it was the night before the exam. Especially when you have no idea of what is in your books, I mean literally! Antennas and Propagation. That was all I knew a night prior to the main exam of the final year. Long ago I had heard the saying, 'with great power comes great responsibilities'. In engineering terms it got bent to, 'with great pressure, comes great packs of cigarettes'. That was mandatory every night before the main exam. We were not among the front benchers who attended the college regularly, respecting the attendance sheet, happened to read regularly, spoke to respected professors in case of self-generated doubts to let them help a little extra in the practical examinations. We rather belonged to the Miss Shivani family (most of the engineering guys do).

So we were all set with our tools – a large pack of Classic Milds, dozens of Red Bull cans and Miss Shivani. And the four of us locked ourselves in the room until next morning. Waiting outside the room was a beefy guy with our cell phones and few more Milds. That is what they do when the question paper is leaked a night before the exam. You got the paper, you surrender yourself to a locked room and no cell phones unless you are done taking the test the next morning. Until then it was all books.

Meanwhile, before we got the question paper in our hands, one of my friends, Sameer, who also happened to be my junior said he'd have to leave to meet some seniors who had called him regarding some matter. Every next hour 'some matter' knocked the door of engineering students, and whether or not we cared enough for electronics and communication, we definitely did to fix every circuit of problems that belonged to almost anyone in our link.

We studied till seven in the morning and when we were almost close to looking like mules, we got ready to leave for the exam.

It went amazingly well. I mean after six months of wavering and one night of marathon reading, we had nailed it!

We were back by the evening and it was party time. After every exam, which mostly happened to be nothing less than great, the story was set – all beer no tear (sometimes whiskey too)!

So we started drinking. I was already two pegs down when I realized that Sameer wasn't back. I asked the others if they knew about the 'matter' he had mentioned. They told me that he had had a conversation with the seniors who hang around the campus and they had called him for a talk. I wasn't too clear what sort of a 'talk' they were talking about, but I continued to drink. Another two down, and we settled down relaxed and happy.

Kick phase. The first phase of being high. That's when you are two pegs down, and by the grace of Mother Black Label, tipsy. Then comes the second phase when you are four pegs down and euphoria sets in. In most cases this is when we start blabbering out our emotions, feel extremely happy and everything in the world seems to be 'just right'. That's the euphoric phase. Then hits the third one when you are six pegs or more down and the love of Lady Label is showered all at once upon you. This is the phase when one recalls their past affairs and most random phone calls are attempted: the moaning phase. People happen to cry, weep and do insane stuff in this phase. Unless you are a master of handling the three of them, you may have a footfall before reaching the fourth level, because the fourth is the master's level. It's after seven pegs or more that you have lost it all. We call it the idiosyncratic phase. You belong to a different world and nothing around you can stop you from doing what you wish to and that's when the world's nastiest stories take place. But we are almost – not even close to it.

So, by the time we were four down I got a call on my phone. It was Sameer on the other end.

"Sir, where are you?" he enquired in a tizzy.

"Sir! Where are *you*? We are four pegs down and waiting for you…"

"I need you to come here," he interrupted me.

"Why, what's wrong? Is everything okay?"

"Umm… I am at this senior's place and they need you here. There is a small issue."

Then he explained that they had a dispute, the details of which are hazy but I remember him mentioning some girl – seniors-talks-ditching-double dating – and that was pretty much I could recall from his story.

I assured him I'd be with him in a bit. I discussed the thing with rest of the guys and then we made a plan – to drink some more.

And so we continued drinking by the time we reached the third stage, although we were not in such a bad shape yet! It was around one in the morning when I got a call. We didn't budge till two.

Finally, as the the clock struck two, we decided to go and check on Sameer. I used to have an Enfield then. We roared into the enemy's territory with that bazooka. The guy inside was senior to me, Mr Rajak. We were four and they were – God! I don't remember exactly but yes, definitely more than us.

Strutting with confidence, I said to their leader, "I guess you wanted us here... so you have us here, what now?"

"So it's you that the chicken made such a big deal about. You are his 'sir'? I see, Mr Vikram."

"Where is Sameer by the way?" I asked sniffing his absence in the room.

"You wish to get kicked right away or should we fix a time to it?" Rajak said.

"You wish to tell me of Sameer's location right away or should we fix a time?"

"He had his share, baby. He made a lot of noise about being associated with you. He has said a lot of stuff about my girl and he has probably got his answer," he mocked and turned to another senior, Tapan, from his group. "He mentioned that you will knock me down, I would like to see that happening!"

"Sir, I guess there is some misunderstanding. Sameer is a silly boy. I am sure he must have crossed the line. Let's not take it there. We don't want any fights," I said bravely while inside I was scared shit.

Damn it Sameer! God knows what you have said!

"Really! You think you'll get out of this so easily? I said that Sameer has got his share, where would you like to get started? Too much confidence that bastard has about you, I just want to tell him who's the king here," saying that he slapped me hard.

"Are you insane?" I cried nursing my jaw.

"I'm sorry, didn't know you were expecting some sanity here!"

Mithil, my Gujju friend knocked him down as he lifted his hand to slap me again.

"Listen, I told you we are not interested in fighting with you guys. Just tell us where Sameer..." and before I could finish, the next thing I saw in front of me gives me chills till date. I crashed down to the ground from the highs of the third phase.

Sweat ran through my temple and there was stark silence in the room. We were all still, a gun pointed at us.

"So, you think you are too smart?" said Tapan, pointing the gun at me. That was the day when I thought that the game is over. I may never be able to see the next morning.

This is it? I'll be shot here and what will my parents be told? That I was six pegs, 360ml down, fighting for a cause that I know nothing about, for a friend who doesn't exist in the scene with people I have never spoken to before? Son-of-a-bitch, above all: I am still a virgin. What would Kanika think about all this? I can't die single. How disgraceful!

We all were drunk, more or less, and that was why there was no chance for anyone but myself to really think. The trigger could have been pulled at any time. I stood there mum with my hands in the air. Saying anything at that point would have gone against me. I kneeled down without a word. And since no word had made enough sense to them, I began crying. Not yelling on top of my voice, but weeping like a kid.

Rajak's ego was boosted as he smirked at me. Everyone stood confused at their positions. I silently wished for some movement, but nothing came from either side for very long.

Mayank from my gang walked up to check on me while Mithil and Ravindra talked the seniors into some closure.

"Get your asses off here, you son-of-whores and make sure you don't turn back," saying this he kept the revolver down and that was when Mithil took charge and hit him hard in his nuts.

...and like they say, there was no looking back then!

We broke into what looked like an action sequence from a cheap Hindi movie where we used almost all the props in our lane.

One punch after the other, and one slang after the other came out from me. I was a walking dictionary of 'mother-sister' slangs. I went a little extra into the character then. Forget mother-sister, I came up with a whole 'ST-SC' list of insults as the guy I was doing belonged to ST/SC class.

We fought the bulls out of the bullies and departed to our place.

By four in the morning, we had lost all our energies to figure out what we had done and we crashed as soon as we reached home.

The next day our hangovers didn't allow us to open our eyes. At around noon I was washing my Enfield when I noticed a police officer walking towards me.

"Mr Vikram?" he asked me in suspicion.

"What is it?"

"Where is the gun?"

A chill ran down my spine.

I was driven to the police station. Somewhere I had in mind that everything would be okay as soon as I explained everything so I kept calm.

"IPC 420, section 3(1) SC/ST act: abusing someone by his caste name, IPC section 506: Threatening to kill somebody, IPC Section 504: Using abusive language," he thundered as I sat there numb.

Looking at the two beasts who stood in front of me, Tapan and Rajak, I said, "Sir, there is a mistake. I did not make any attempt to murder or threaten anyone," I said rising up from my chair.

"Mistake, are you trying to say that we made a mistake? Oh, and before I forget, where is the gun?"

"I don't know what gun you are talking about. I had no gun. I admit we had a fight, I beat them, but that is all. The gun you are talking about was with them. It was theirs!"

"Section 452 IPC: carrying a gun with you illegally."

"There is no gun. It was just a hand in hand fight. I don't have a gun."

"And how would you explain abusing Tapan in the name of his caste?"

"I'll apologize for that. I was drunk and not in my senses. I am sorry."

"In fact, my friend Sameer is missing since last night. I would like you to ask them what they did to him," I said pointing at Rajak

"I have mentioned to you earlier he had left right after we talked. We have no clue what happened to him thereafter."

"No, I don't buy that. You have definitely done something in between. They know where he is!"

"You don't have to worry about Sameer, worry about yourself. You have no idea what kind of trouble you are in, boy" the inspector said, resting his butt on the table.

I had nowhere to go then. I begged to be let out of the mess, offered the possible bribe and did all that was possible at that moment.

Only till the next thing that I could hear him saying, "IPC Section 307: Attempt to murder. I may take away your degree, kid."

I froze. My ability to think became impaired. I managed to file an F.I.R. against the two for Sameer's disappearance and took permission to walk out of the police station.

I had controlled myself and tried to recall all the events of the night and the day. I reached home only to find Sameer there.

"Where the hell were you?" I yelled, less happy and more troubled finding him there. "I have lodged an FIR, thinking you had gone missing."

"Missing? Who, I? Sir, I got slightly drunk and fell asleep at Raunak's place."

"What about the fight?"

"What fight?"

"Rajak didn't beat you?"

"There was no fight, I just sang your praises so he wanted to see you. That bitch Ankita dumped me in front of him. There was nothing to fight over after that. So I just walked out. Did you talk to him?"

I wish I had a gun at that time and I did not even mind being slapped with Section 452. Thank goodness, however, that Sameer was fine. Like they say that no one can touch your butt when your time is right. Maybe the time was good for me then. We talked ourselves out of the mess, of course after a lot of bribes and an intact degree. I swear to God to listen to every 'matter' carefully the next time before getting involved!

Drive-In-Sanity

©

There is a very mystic correlation between a crazy night and a forgetful morning; the latter is mostly followed by the former.

I woke up in my bed; it was morning. I spit out a tooth.

Oh gosh! It's my tooth!

It was my twenty-second birthday and all I remember from the previous night was saying, "I want one."

I stood in my bed looking at my own tooth and feeling the empty socket in my gums, wondering what exactly had happened the night before.

It was the 13th of May 2012. At four in the morning of my birthday, my friend and I were hovering aimlessly in a Maruti Ritz which had a number plate of Punjab in the streets of Indore city. No – we weren't up on my birthday morning to head to a church, we were up all night celebrating and the night didn't seem to be over for us. Although we did eventually head to a church a few hours later, but we'll get there later.

I would rewind the whole scene hours later from this and till date I am quite foggy about what exactly happened that night, but here is what I could recollect.

2.00 a.m.

In a local pub of Indore named O2, we all stood against the bar awaiting fire shots. We cheered one another for each shot of tequila downed.

"To Ayesha, happy birthday," my friends cheered, and that was probably the last thing that I clearly remember. After that, all I remember was a toilet, some toilet paper, and Sasha puking. The worst part about my group was that we were all girls, but the best part was that we still had an all time chauffer who never got drunk enough and could always drive us back safely. Unfortunately, that chauffer was me, who never got enough room to get wasted even on her birthday night... morning.

So after 2 pegs, the job I was left with was taking care of the other ankles in high heels, staggering their way to the loo. In most cases it was Sasha to lose consciousness. And since it was my birthday, as a regular episode of an after party soap, they got high. Random guys hugged them, kissed them and cried for them, and with much help from them, we managed to get back home safely.

Sasha was my roommate in those days and we stayed in a rented room. The society had accepted us coming home at any hour in almost any possible condition: I know because we had tried almost all of them so far. All we needed to manage was the five-feet-eight-inches lady lying on the back seat of our car, because all that was understood from her was the name of the guy whom she got drunk with last, and luckily, he was in our car too. I do not remember his name but let's say his name was 'I know everything' since he used that phrase a lot when he spoke.

Sasha was too drunk to be asked to get out of the car and go up to her room.

I-Know-Everything helped Raina with Sasha and asked me to park the car while they cleared the mess.

They moved upstairs. That was apparently the end of that night. My birthday night was over, just like that. It was like any other Saturday night. I did not really enjoy going to clubs. It was for people who enjoyed dancing; the crowd made it impossible to step on the floor. Or for people who preferred getting insanely drunk; that was a way out of the monotonous. Or for those who were hoping to get an opportunity to go out and find themselves a date for Sunday evening, or probably get wasted, make guilt-free revelations and involve in bacchanalia and loose oneself.

I, on the other hand, didn't feel excited about any of these. Eleena and I stayed in the car for a while.

Eleena was not a close friend but one of my friends' friend and my senior in college. The night wasn't too great for both of us. Both of us were among the tshatshkes at the bar who preened at themselves and then at happy couples.

There is a rule in night clubs: either everyone is a couple in the gang or no one is. I was pretty much single; Sasha and Raina had a date, always. Eleena was the odd one out who was in a relationship, yet had boyfriend issues, always. So it was usually Eleena and I who shared the space, literally.

She lay back dozy on the rear seat as I turned around. *So, that's it? My 22nd birthday night would end up with a roaring Godzilla puking back at home and a few shots of lemonade, few more of salt water – and then more puke.* I didn't wish to end it there and before I could say anything, Eleena said, "I don't wish to end up here."

Both of us shared a look and before we could discuss anything, she jumped ahead at the front seat and said, "Let's go."

My car veered off the parking and the gear was pulled.

We didn't know where to head next. The party was over and we were done with clubs. We pulled out a bottle of Bacardi from the back of my seat. When it came to clubbing, we always had a policy: drink partially before entering the party, it saved money! But this time it went a little against us. But the good news was that we were not done yet, nor was the night!

3.00 a.m.

She made 2 pegs for each of us and we drove aimlessly on the streets of Indore, half drunk, in a car with a number plate of Punjab...but we will get there in few hours from now. We cheered and toasted to the beginning of the night.

Eleena uttered, "I miss Atul."

A research by NACS (National Alcohol Consuming Society) says that ninety percent of people talked about their boyfriends/ girlfriends/ crushes when they got drunk, five percent talked about their wives, and the remaining five about how they got addicted to the habit out of bankruptcy.

One of the ninety percent was seated next to me blabbering. "He never understands me. He always has something or the other to quarrel about. I mean, you tell me how does it work?"

"Yeah... It doesn't," I nodded in concordance.

"See, even you feel the same. I asked him to come with me to the party, but he has no time for me. I always ask him out, but seems like he has time for everything else but me..."

Things seem hazy and what I remember from a few minutes later was her saying, "I mean, you tell me how it works."

"Yeah...it doesn't," I shrugged in agreement again.

And since both of us were drunk, neither of us fairly remembers the talk that we had, but the last we remembered was that we ran out of chips.

"No more chips?" I yelled over the music.

"I know. I am starving!"

"Me too, what should we do now?"

"I don't know. Atul always got me chips…" she began and she reached for her phone to call Atul. After a long discussion, I caught Eleena throwing her phone at the dash board of the car before bursting into tears.

"Why are you crying? Eleena, stop crying."

"What have I done? He always hangs up on me. He is mad at me because I am drunk."

"Is that even a point? I mean he gets drunk whenever he wants to." I said this though I didn't even know what Atul looked like!

"No, he is a Jain, and he doesn't even talk about drinking to me," Eleena sobbed.

"But he is the reason why you are drunk. I mean would it not be easier for him to keep you from drinking by being around than telling you off on the phone?"

"Right…right…that's what I mean. You tell me how does it work?"

"Yeah…it doesn't."

"I must call him again."

"Listen Eleena, may be this is not the time. You are drunk and he doesn't wish to listen to you. Better put your phone down. If he has to talk to you, he will call you."

"You are right. I have cried enough over him. Now I won't call him anymore," she said to my relief. "Instead, I must go to his place and confront him directly."

"What? No, we are not going to his place."

4.00 a.m.
En route Atul's place

It was a quite a feat that we found our way to Atul's at that hour.

"I will tell that bastard whom has he been messing with."

We both careened upstairs. Atul lived in an apartment with one of his friends...but hang on, we were not at Atul's place then. It was his friend's place but we don't quite remember why we were there. Maybe Atul told Eleena on the phone that he was there...maybe she knew it...whatever.

We knocked loudly and since the door was not locked, we walked right into a little argument between Vishal and some girl, most probably his girlfriend.

"Eleena, what are you doing here?" Vishal said looking baffled.

The girl next to him asked equally baffled, "Who is she?"

After all the clarifications and introductions, we ended up rounding a few more drinks. And while Eleena was busy being the peace-maker, I managed to get some chips from the shelf.

A little beer, a few fags of the hookah and we forgot what had really got us there. Few minutes later, Vishal and his girl were enjoying a game of monopoly with us, "You girls want a game? I will show you a game," she roared throwing two dices in a row and we all cheered another shot at it.

The night did not turn out to be bad as we thought it would. Eleena and I stood on their bed and danced our hearts out. In no time Vishal's girl joined us and started stripping. She pulled off her jacket and threw it at Vishal. That was all they needed to patch up and they left the room soon.

Loaded with chips and dips, we were back in our car.

5.00 a.m.

The music was loud and Atul was out of our heads. We were talking of the bar. People on the roads were returning from parties. Both Eleena and I believed that clubbing was overrated and the pre and post clubbing scenes were much more fun. The sneaking down the apartment, the pre-booze time in the car, the hitting back drunk on the roads, walking past the cops at three in the morning on the streets and pretending to be normal, the mint flavoured drags and slurping cheese Maggi at 4.00 a.m. as we tried to sort the mess. After a party, there was always a mess.

We were hungry again. The best part about Indore city is that at any hour of the day, there is some food stall open. People are real foodies. We found ourselves a Maggi and tea stall by the side of the road. People who were back from parties were stuffing themselves. We checked out the place for a minute – there were all men there. Too bad, we couldn't stop there. Tipsy and wearing eight inches long skirts…we would have drawn a lot of unwanted attention. All that said, we didn't have any money with us so it would have been futile. We continued driving.

Eleena pulled down the window and put her head out to feel the breeze on her face.

"This is exactly what you want after a good drink," she said turning back, "or before one," and picked another pint. "I couldn't forget that at O2."

I quirked, "So there was a guy?"

"Ya…he walked up to me asking me my name, where I was from and so on. He was the guy. I wish I had made a move with him. Damn Atul!"

"And back we go again. Did he by any chance have a single friend as well?"

"Maybe. Actually yes, he did. I remember him saying something about it."

"Why didn't you tell me there? We could have totally made a move; I mean at least dance moves."

And then all the powers of the universe united to make a move in our favour. A black Audi Q3 crossed our way. We made quick eye contact with the two guys inside it. They honked signalling us to stop. It occurred to us that the guy driving it was the one who had walked up to Eleena in the bar. And so we stopped.

"Hi!" One of them got out of the car.

"This is the same guy...what do we do now?" Eleena said nervously.

"Hi." We replied in unison.

"It occurred to us that you guys wanted to get down at that tea stall but could not."

"If you want we can get some food for you. It is just a corner away. You guys wait here and we will be back in no time."

"Sure," I shrugged, blushing a little.

"No. It's okay, don't bother," Eleena said.

"It's not a problem, we will be back soon. Don't worry, just stay here."

One weird thing happened before they left.

"Excuse me, do you have a friend?" I asked.

"Yes, I have a few of them, why?"

"I want one," I staggered back into the car before I could realize what I had said.

After loitering for some time on the streets, we got ourselves some cheese Maggi and tea, and as gentlemen, they did not expect us paying them. We did not find any other thing more interesting than that, and so we left them with our fake details and moved on. The night was on again. We drank, we ate, we sung, and drove. We were so drunk that we did not realize where and how far we had driven. The only thing we knew was that in some time, we were forty kilometres away from the city.

Indore is a pretty compressed city. The town seems to end within a diameter of ten kilometres. Before we noticed the green board, we were far away from the city and the icing to the cake was that the fuel tank of the car was nearly empty.

"Ayesha, where are we?" Eleena asked peering at the road.

"I have no idea."

We were apparently on a highway and every other car, truck, bike and even a dog crossing our way looked menacing. We had no idea of how we landed up on that road and no idea of what we'd do next.

"What do we do?"

"I don't know," I said, still driving.

"I think you should turn the car around."

"I know, but I am too scared. Can you see any vehicles coming? We are on a highway. You never turn on the highway," I retorted.

It was daybreak and the road was clear, so we reversed. We drove almost twenty kilometres in reverse gear that morning before we could turn around. And only then we found ourselves a fuel pump. It seemed like everything was going in our favour. I got down in my four inches long heels and eight inches long skirt. Who needs cash? Adding to that, the fuel guy happened to be really gullible and cute. He kept looking at me smiling.

"Full tank," I ordered.

"That would be one thousand eight hundred rupees," he smiled.

I brought my assets to full use then. I pretended to look into my wallet and wailed about forgetting my cash.

"Oh no! There is no cash, what should I do now? I have no fuel at all, could you please let me take this now and I will come back tomorrow and pay you the full amount?"

"That is not happening, ma'am. I am afraid I have to re-pull the oil."

"How about you take my watch for now; it is worth four thousand rupees. I will come back tomorrow, give you the money and take my watch back. What say?"

"It's against the rule, but since you look so cute and pretty, I don't mind waiting."

He smiled at me and I handed my watch to him. Everything was arranged. Luck seemed to be in our favour that morning.

Before I left, I turned around coyly, "By the way, did I mention that you look like Sachin, the cricketer."

The guy blushed and smiled as I walked up to my car, "Like your curls."

"Guess we are all set for our endless drive," I grinned at Eleena

6.30 a.m.

Our car stopped at few kilometres from the fuel pump, "Son of a bitch pulled out the fuel!"

Eleena did not look very well. She was going to throw up at any moment. We were in the middle of the road; there was nowhere we could head to. At that moment, I saw a church across the lane. Eleena and I walked up to the church as sombre as we could look. There were a lot of people gathered for the Sunday morning service. We sat on the back bench.

We sat singing hymns with them for around an hour before Raina reached. I don't know how she came to know about our location, but before I could interrogate her, Eleena threw up as we walked out of the church. And while Raina went to help her, I stumbled upon something and woke up on my bed spitting out a tooth.

6.00 p.m.

It was evening and the four of us were sitting with bad headaches and a large mug of coffee each, reminiscing the incredible night. The night was more than incredible. But there were a few changes to the story that I recalled.

It seems that Eleena had mistakenly exchanged her phone with the guy who walked up to her at the pub and kept receiving his calls all the way, assuming Atul was on the other end, which is why the guy was so mad at her.

When we reached Vishal's place, we know why Atul was not there. She had never really had a talk with Atul. We danced on the bed and played a few dices at monopoly, when Vishal's girl stripped off her jacket in angst at him and the next thing we remember her saying, "You girls want a game? I will show you a game," and kicked our dices off the board. We stole some food and sneaked out later.

The two guys saw us from the stall and followed us to collect their cell phone. We were so starved by then that I asked him to give me the Maggi which he was already halfway through.

Of course the only thing that I remember clearly was me saying, "I want one," which happened exactly the way I remembered it. The only difference was that the guys left disgusted with us.

The fuel pump guy...well, there was no fuel pump in real but a hoarding of some oil advertisement with Sachin on it. Yes,

I gave away my watch to a banner! This was why our vehicle stopped one kilometre from there. Meanwhile, Eleena regained her senses and called Raina.

The worst was what happened at the church. People preened at us as though we were zombies walking in, and for the next one hour we were stared at by the entire hall as we sang the hymns aloud.

I threw up as we walked out of the church and fell into my own puke...the rest is a dentist's story.

But the one little detail that I still take pride on was me driving in reverse gear for twenty kilometres straight. Which was corrected to two blocks and the fact added to it was that we never drove that far from the city. The sign board was of a resort that was forty kilometres from that point. But I don't buy it yet.

It was the best birthday night we had ever had, in spite of losing my expensive watch to a poster guy! It was the night when Eleena and I became best friends and I am still looking forward to getting my reverse drive registered in the Limca Book of Records!

Kicking the Butt

The day of her wedding is the most special day in a girl's life. Everything goes as per her wish. She is the queen. The queen needs it to be perfect: the perfect flower arrangement, perfect make-up, perfect catering, perfect appreciation for her hairdo and even the perfect guest list.

Have you ever seen a bride to be breaking into a fight at her own wedding? And not like a decent argument, but a brawl that may get a million hits if it goes on YouTube?

It was February 1999 at the time when I, Sanya Rhoda, was the bride and this is the story of how we kicked that unwanted guest from my wedding.

Before I begin, I must tell you that the video did get on YouTube and it did get a million views. Soon we were being offered ads to post on our video, but we will get to that later.

Before I start the story, it is important to know why this guest was so unwanted that we needed to kick him out of the wedding venue one night before the big day.

To explain that, let's skip to the day when the preparations to the big day were on. The caterers were chosen, the venue was booked and the photographer was picked. He was working with my company. Nikul would do it for less than half of what the other photographers were charging. He was a friend and a colleague and in a desperate need to make some extra money. We were revising the guest list as we wrote out invitation cards to everyone on that list of 500 guests.

There were uncles I didn't like, relatives I barely knew, friends who were not even declared friends by me, but their names were there because their parents attended my parent's wedding. Though I am quite sure they would never say anything good about me; not even on the day when I am the winning candidate of the Lokpal elections, for real.

But I had no issues with anyone being there and all were welcome, until I stumbled upon this one name which I hated – Mahendra Rajani.

It's not that the name came as a big surprise to me, but I was not glad to see it. The memories I had of this guy came flooding back. I can never forget what happened between us and the worst part was that it didn't make any difference to him. His filthy face was ever smiling and he pretended like nothing had ever happened.

Mahendra Rajani was my mother's first cousin's husband, but his role in the family was more than that. He was one of the best sons-in-law our family had ever had; in fact, any family could ever have. He had no son-in-law ego issues, he never had clashes with anyone, he used to be the favourite of the youngsters, and of course, people of his age. He had a great sense of humour and also seemed to never grow old. Any girl would dream of a life partner like him. He was a darling to all. If kids didn't agree with the elders, they called Mahendra to speak to them; if there were any disputes to be resolved, Mahendra would always be there to fix the situation; and if the youngsters wished to stay up partying for extra hours, they would call him to talk to the elders on their behalf. He was a giver, a saviour, and a charmer. In other words, the most awesome person in our extended family.

By now I might have left you wondering about what exactly was my problem with the super-uncle that I would not have him attend my wedding.

To explain that, I may have to rewind the story a few years back when we were at my cousin's wedding in Delhi. It was one of those events in our family where everyone related – more or less – would show up. Some would show up as a matter of guilt for not attending weddings in the past, some would show up because it was the time when a lot of us were young enough to tie the knot and may get lucky to find a nice girl or guy in the symposium, some would show up since it was summers and easy to make big holiday plans, while other would come just because everyone else would be showing up.

It was a big reunion for all the cousins after a long time. We had all grown up pretty much since our last reunion.

Mahendra Uncle was the father of two kids himself – a son and a daughter. We were all of the same age group. We were all staying together for two days. The wedding celebrations were over and all the cousins had gathered for the last night, while all the elders were nursing their ankles, which they had hurt on the beats of the no-music Sindhi songs that were sung throughout the wedding for five days straight.

But among all other elders, Mahendra Uncle stayed back with us. We played dumb charades till one in the morning. He was the leader of the opposing team. We played hide-n-seek at five in the morning and he was present. we played hidden treasure at six, and yes, he was still there.

At around four in the morning, we decided to play dark room and I wish I had not joined in. The lights were put off and the curtains were pulled. There was a dim light in the room coming in from the windows. We all hid in different places – some in the closet, some under the study table and a lot of them inside the blanket on the bed. I went down in one corner behind the chair while Mahendra Uncle hid in the other corner of the same wall. While everyone else was busy hooting the seeker, Mahendra Uncle crawled into my space. I stepped aside to hide my face when he leaned on my shoulder. It felt uncomfortable so I stepped away. He moved towards me and leaned on my arms. I didn't know what exactly was happening, I shrugged his hands off me and wrapped my arms around myself. In some time I could feel him leaning heavily and pushing his body on my body and kissing my arms. I shoved him back and before I could shout, the lights were switched on and everyone in room was booing.

Mahendra Uncle stood up to boo with the rest of them and I sat there puzzled and wondering exactly what had happened a minute ago. The next round began and I decided to concentrate on the game. The lights were switched off once again and this time I hid inside the blanket with the other kids to make sure I did not get cornered. We wrestled for space on the bed for a few minutes before the next round. When everyone went quiet in the room, I felt someone tickling me down there. I shook my legs and it happened again for a few seconds, until the bed broke because of the weight of the children. The lights were switched on and I saw Mahendra Uncle sneaking out of the cover.

I did not know what was going on. I was infuriated as much as I was appalled.

Just then I asked Sakshi, his daughter, sitting right in front of him, "Sakshi, what's your age?"

"Nineteen," she replied smiling as I turned to Mahendra Uncle the very next moment. He kept mum for a while and then he looked away. I kept staring at him for the next few minutes, but he avoided me.

An hour later when we were playing hide-n-seek, he came behind me to the construction site of the venue. Before I could turn my back, he apologized to me with a grin. It was as though he was mocking me. I moved away scowling at him without saying a word.

I had a few hiccups before I could forget the anagram but while penning down his name, my heart wished I did not have to have him in my wedding. I licked the envelope and stacked it with the rest of the pile.

He never put his eyes down after that. He talked about me to the others, walked around proud as a peacock behaving like nothing ever happened. There was no repentance. He must have done it to the others as well. It seemed like it was no big deal. Yet, the fact remained, that everyone liked him in the family and vindicating him of anything like this would put me in a spot instead.

While jotting down the other names, I thought what kind of a jerk he was! After all this time, how hypocritical it would be to face him and face him with a smile, shake hands with him, have him during the sangeet to dance with me, to receive his blessings and to bow down to him...ugh!

"He cannot be there at my wedding," I said aloud.

I didn't intend to make a scene of that one small incident. In fact, I completely wished to erase it from my life, but the thought that he would be present at my wedding was not that pleasing. I had no problem if he was there, but the fact that he was not even one percent ashamed of what he had done was getting on my nerves.

Everyone on the dining table was quiet.

"Who, who cannot be there at your wedding?" my mother engaged with a pair of scissors and glue asked me.

"Mahendra Rajani," I asserted.

Then I explained the whole story, and to my astonishment, it wasn't as tough as I thought it would be. I finished my story in a few decent sentences and waited for them to react to it.

My mother could be horrified about the whole thing and she could be on my side. She could get emotional and console me and ask me to forget what had happened. She could side with me but convince me about the fact that he is family after all. But when she finally did speak, she said something no girl could ever expect from her own mother.

"Why did you have to be around him?" she uttered after the longest pause.

"Why did I have to be around him? You are questioning me after all this, seriously? I was one of those kids; he was the only adult playing with us. If there is one person you should question, it should be him, not me," I slammed.

"It's okay. He did what he did. Why are you making a big deal about it? Just be alert the next time. We cannot allow relations crumble because of this. It happens," saying that, she turned away.

I didn't know how to react to that, but like I would have done to any reverse solution from my mother, I put it under the bed and forgot about it.

The wedding was in seven days. I was rather excited for the big day that was to come in a week's time.

In an ideal Sindhi wedding, there is something called Saatth. It is one of the rituals involving a minimum of seven women. They all would winnow wheat grain, sing regional songs, knot the ends of seven stoles, one for each, and bless the bride. It was a very small function at my place with just the ladies from the neighbourhood participating. After it was over, my sister and I were chatting over snacks when she began to talk about Mahendra Uncle.

"You did a great thing coming clean with what happened," she said.

"I know, but how does it matter? At the end, all of it was my mistake to be a part of the games," I retorted.

"Yes, but someone has to break the silence at some point. At least they have a clue about his character now."

"What do you mean someone has to break the silence?" I questioned.

"Well, let's say you are not the only victim. The same thing happened to me as well a few years ago."

And then she narrated how in a party he had said irrelevant things to her; at a picnic to the water park, he tried making a move in a closed slide and in the pool later; in the car he would ogle at her from the rear view mirror and would child lock the doors to stop her when everyone else had got out of the car. I was flabbergasted. The nerve of the man to do what he had done, and all the while posing as the best son-in-law a family could ever have. I decided to tell my dad.

I thought maybe it was not the best idea to reveal it to him, for he didn't like my mother's family too much and this would give him just another reason to dislike them. However, I found out that he was not mad at my mother at all. Few minutes later I discovered that he was not mad at Mahendra Uncle either. And few moments after that I was more than amazed when he called me an extrovert. The word was 'extrovert'.

"I always tell you to play safe, but do you ever listen to me? The world outside is dangerous. Blame yourself for being an extrovert," he uttered.

"Seriously! Your daughters are standing in front of you telling you about a family member harassing them, and all you have to say is that we are extroverts? I mean, what wrong did we do, can you please explain? I was just playing with other kids of my age, he was the odd one out, but we are to be blamed? I mean, seriously," I shook in anger.

"Do you have an answer to why it was you but no one else?" my dad threw a question at me.

"Because I was the eldest of them all, and the others were younger to me."

"Then what were you doing there? If you are the eldest, I expect you to be mature enough."

"Mature? Sunny was there too, and she is elder to me by two years. And what would you say in her case?" I asked turning to my sister, "She wasn't the eldest in the group when it happened."

"You don't understand when I..." my dad tried to argue. I don't even remember what he said next. It was like trying to hit my head against a wall.

I had well imagined what my dad would have said to me if I ever introduced my boyfriend and told him that I wished to marry him, "I would like to see his parents someday."

I showed up with my mark sheet with an F remark, "What went wrong?"

I had been suspended for a day from school for trying to bunk a day. "This has happened to me before, but you took a bigger leap."

But the task at hand, to teach this family member a lesson, was a big one.

So I had to interrupt him, "You know what, it is okay. I completely understand. Let it go," I turned my back at them.

I sat down crossing my legs on the water tank at the terrace enjoying a cigarette and pondering over the past and the present. I wondered how similar this act of moral policing is to that of smoking.

We already know how cancerous cigarettes have been for man. There had been documentaries, advertisements and statutory warnings through all the possible mediums, and despite the 'tobacco leads to cancer' ads, it makes no difference to anyone but only to the tobacco industry for getting added users with every commencing high school session. Then there is the case of the hookah. It is possible that hookah leads to cancer – definitely possible – but less likely than cigarettes. People don't give much importance about banning cigarettes. Smoking a hookah is a health menace, but only because it has lately been in trend, it builds a lot more smoke than the usual butt. It is an attraction for youngsters to try and that makes the government want to ban it.

Similarly, discussing some man's fault isn't as smoky and as enticing as a girl's would be.

He had touched me in a dark room while we were playing. In the presence of fifteen kids. And it appeared that he did it just because he wished to touch me. He is a father of a girl as old as me. He was probably aware that no one would tolerate something like that. Maybe a kid, but not a grown-up like me. He did not approach me with words to have a stirring interlocution, neither did he force me. I am still amazed and wonder what goes on in the mind as one does these things. Just a touch? Just an idea of being able to 'try' to get a feel of a younger girl? Or is it the casual idea of selling betel nuts while no one cares about who's chewing?

I wonder how my playing hide-n-seek with my cousins and enjoying it without bothering the presence of some "one" can convict me. Yet, the sheesha is banned if there's any complaint – even once.

I guess everyone waits for cancer, and until that occurs, there is no kicking of the butt.

Once again I buried everything under my bed and looked forward to the brighter side of the wedding. The big day had finally arrived.

It was a big fat Sindhi wedding with big fat unreasonably fair Sindhi uncles and aunts all around. We all had gathered at the wedding venue for the second day celebration and that night was the night of the ring ceremony and cocktails. I had settled in the bride's room along with my mother. The wedding was to take place the very next day, and as per the Sindhi culture, the wedding was to be during the day, and the reception at night.

The guests kept trickling in until we finally exchanged rings on the podium. This was the happiest day of my life. I was getting married to my best friend and that was all I ever wanted. The ceremonies were performed, we had cut the cake and the bottle of champagne was uncorked.

Amid all the celebrations, Mahendra Uncle had arrived on the stage to wish us. But I was okay with it, as I was too happy to care about anything else. He wished us, made us have a bite of the cake and went back to join the others. Drinks-dining-dancing. It was a perfect night. The minor imperfections came to be perfect over wine.

As my eyes swept over all the guests, I was surprised to see Mahendra Uncle leaning on someone. And the 'someone' was none other than his own niece Mini, who happened to be younger than his own daughter. I didn't give it much thought considering the amount of alcohol I had consumed, but once again the past was in front of me when I saw him next to her during the entire night.

The swine!

After dinner, all of us went back into our respective rooms. I wrapped my evening gown and got inside my blanket to have my pre-wedding beauty slumber. I tossed around for a while but Uncle Mahendra's face wouldn't leave my mind. After a few minutes of turning and tossing on my bed, I went out for a walk.

"A toast to your last night as a virgin," one of my friends raised a toast to me while we sat out in the balcony with a bottle of wine.

Now I am not much of a drinker but that night, I will always be glad of making myself those two pegs. I owe them big time for what happened next. It would never have happened if there was no toast to me that night.

2 pegs ke baad I revealed Mahendra Uncle's history to my friends, "I told him off. I made him to apologize for his actions because what he did a decade ago was the first round and I am sure this wasn't just the second. There must have been a lot of targets in between these years."

And after realizing that to wait for cancer to kick the butt is not the way out, maybe kicking the butt right away was the legit one.

I called Uncle Mahendra to the room and welcomed him with a glass of scotch. I looked at his innocent face and thought about how he had been fooling everyone with it all these years. I made myself a drink and swaggered towards him to say, "I have something for you."

Two kicks straight in his nards and we left slamming the door behind our backs.

"Remember this before you propose to play 'dark room' with Mini," I grinned and gulped down the third peg.

Male infidelity has become a common fact; so much so that it makes no sense to talk about it anymore. The audience is fed up of the *'itna tar bahut bimar'* commercials before every featured presentation at halls.

Mahendra Uncle never showed up during the wedding, but he did so at the reception, only with an inappropriate gait.

So I may not have chosen to speak up. My friends continued to be polite or quiet rather than jeopardizing their social and professional network. So the hookah stays mum. But did the banning of hookah from the bars really help? Well, we all know it is back in our homes; we still do consume it – just silently.

We stay mum, we stay foolish. And as we all know, the cigarette industry only flourishes!

Rosita in the Bar

It was six in the morning when Uncle Fransis woke up to his closet wide open in his room and all the gold missing from the jewellery box. Some cash was missing from his wardrobe as well. The next morning the news was between everyone's tea cups and saucers. Fransis's daughter, Rosita, had eloped with Savio, a lad from the neighbouring town. Fransis was well known in the district of North Goa and any important decision in the society was preceded by his consent. After the incident he disowned his daughter and never turned to her again.

Years later, Cortalim, Goa

A girl was sitting in a black coat with a glass of soda placed in front of her. Her black gloves lay beside it. She looked around at the people in the bar, cheering, blabbering, fighting with the bartender for a last drink and enjoying the high. At three in the morning, she would make the payment and gather her gloves. Before moving out she covered her face with a black stole and sneaked away quietly.

At around four she returned home and locked the doors stealthily to avoid waking me up from sleep. She stepped in furtively towards the hanger resting on the wall outside the room and after hanging her coat on it, she got under my blanket beside me and went to sleep. I don't know if she even really slept at that time or just pretended to so that I'd not question her.

Often I used to hear her crying on her pillow, but I knew that it was something she did not want to discuss with me, so I never questioned her.

Rosita had lost her husband. She has been living with me in the town of Cortalim ever since. She had no one except me, but I always knew that deep down she was very alone. She had been with Savio for ten years after they got married. Rosita was two months pregnant when she had left her parent's home and got married. They had been together for ten years until the clock for Savio ran faster than for the rest. He fell ill and it only got worse with time. He had lost himself into drinking. He used to move out to drink in the evening and only showed up the next morning. It continued for a while until one morning when he never returned. For the world, he was dead; but Rosita never accepted that.

Savio's death came as a big loss to her. She knew that he wasn't doing any better, but he was all she had. Ever since he passed away, I have never seen her smiling. I have never seen her crying either – not even at his funeral. But it seemed like she was searching for something. I don't know what it was, maybe nothing but Savio everywhere around her. She had no one with her she could call her own. So she came here with me to start anew. I never questioned her about Savio, and she never said anything about him. We were just pillars to support each other.

Rosita made cakes from home for a bakery shop owned by Savio's uncle. Savio had not been doing anything for very long. When she found they were out of food, she started to make cakes and Uncle Robin looked after the shop.

Every morning at seven Rosita would wake me up, make breakfast for me and would send me off to office now that I finally had a job, and then she'd go back to sleep. Later she would make the batter while pouring out some milk for Cinderella. Cinderella was our cat and it had been a gift from Savio. She had grown old by now, but Rosita loved her the way she would have loved her daughter. She would put the cakes in the oven one after the other and in the evening would take them to the shop. For every cake, she was paid a hundred rupees, and that looked pretty good to keep her going even if she hated to face Robin and his daily kvetch over something or the other about her cakes. She couldn't leave until they picked at a bone. It always had to do with something about him making better sales if she added more butter to the cakes.

While heading back home from the bakery, she would buy fish for me and Cinderella. Over dinner, her favourite topics of conversation were about repairing the broken oven or squawking about Uncle Robin's attitude towards her cakes or about Cinderella not having her food properly. I would not bring up office at dinner or even after that, and neither would she. When the clock would strike eleven, she would switch off the lights and lie down beside me pretending to sleep. Then every night, an hour later she would check on and then quietly pull her feet out of the blanket, put on her black coat and cover her face with a stole and would sneak out of the house.

I didn't know for how long she had been doing this until one day when I woke up to go to the bathroom. I noticed she wasn't there beside me. I heard her entering the house. I knew it was not something usual, but I stayed silent and watched her sneaking into the bed beside me once she made sure that I was asleep.

It went on for days, weeks and as long as for a month, but I didn't ask her anything about it. I knew there was something I deserved to know. I worried in case Rosita was in some kind of trouble.

One night I followed her. Cortalim was rather deserted at midnight, but she made her way through the dark and solicited streets carefully. I had no clue where she was headed. Possibly she was secretly meeting someone. A few minutes later I found her entering a bar. *Santosa* it read outside. I stayed outside and watched her go in. She took off her stole after entering the bar. I stood in the parking lot and watched her from outside the window of the bar. Rosita had not realized that I was stalking her. She pulled her gloves off and sat there for a while. Then some time later the waiter brought her a glass of soda and lemons. I waited to see if she would drink as we had never discussed about that. But surprisingly she did not ask for any alcohol. An hour passed by. I hoped for someone to show up. Sitting there while squeezing the lemons into her soda, she looked around her. I kept my eyes stuck on her table. She remained seated, looking around her at every sip of her virgin drink.

A dark, fat man sitting alone with a glass of whiskey constantly stared at her. He was tanked as he gazed at her. I looked at him with a hundred conundrums weaving in my head. What was she so guilty about that she would keep this from me? Rosita kept sitting and sipping from that one glass she started with. There were hardly any women around, only two other than Rosita. Men around her kept peering at her. A few hours passed. She finished her drink, put on her gloves, wrapped herself in the stole and got up to leave. I sprinted homewards and got back under my blanket.

The next night she did the same thing. Years passed by and the routine continued. Rosita kept visiting the bar, sipping her non-alcoholic lemonade and returning. I followed her for a couple of nights. Nothing new happened. Rosita sat there all by herself. No one ever showed up.

"Cinderella has not been drinking her milk for a few days. I think we need to take her to the doctor," Rosita said to me while serving some biryani on my plate. I kept listening to her with half ears.

"Are you listening to me?" Rosita turned to me rubbing her hands against her forehead.

"Yes, yes, I will," I turned to her in agitation.

"What happened? Is everything fine?" she enquired

"Yes, perfect," I said. "There is one thing, however, but I don't know how I should say this," I stammered. "Do you...I mean, is there any..."

"It must be acidity. How many times I tell you not to drink water with your food? And your late night munching habit must stop. Should I give you some medicine?" Rosita reached for a glass of water. "Have you been working too hard these days?" she asked as she handed the glass to me and turned back to the sink filled with dirty dishes.

I gawked at the glass in my hands and the little dough that hung on its edges.

"Where have you been going at night?" I finally blurted.

Rosita had started washing the dishes, and became absolutely still for a moment. There was silence between us and then she continued to scrub.

"I know you have been going somewhere every night. I have seen you. I need to hear it from you."

She kept doing the dishes pretending to be inaudible to me.

"I have seen you visiting that bar. I know you visit a bar every night."

Rosita remained quiet.

"Listen, I know there is something that you have been hiding from me all this time. But your silence won't keep me from it for longer. Sooner or later I will find it out – if not from you then from someone else. And I will," I affirmed.

I stood there watching her chopping the tomatoes, and awaiting a reaction. Her grip on the knife appeared to have loosened down. I watched her chopping aimlessly in wrath until she was finished.

"It's your dad," she said.

Rosita then told me the truth that she had hidden from me for years. She had lost her husband, my dad, in a riot that broke out between Nigerians and a few locals over cocaine. There happened to be a dispute at a rave party in which people were injured. Savio was among the few. Rosita waited for a long time for him. The next morning she filed an FIR. The police couldn't find him anywhere for a week.

"He used to visit that bar very often. Every night he would come half drunk to me and ask for more money. If I refused, he would hit me and take out the little I earned from baking from the wardrobe. In the morning, before you'd wake up, he would return in full consciousness and lie down, regretting what he had done the previous night. He was not a bad man. He was good. I knew him; he was good inside. But alcohol ruined him," Rosita chafed her temple and sobbed against her wrist. "That night, I am sure alcohol was the only reason that got him involved in that mess," she added wiping her hands on her gown.

"The police never found him, nor did they find his body. The locals said they had seen him in that bar for the last time. They wished to close his file and so he was declared dead. His tomb is there in the cemetery where we visit it every year.

"You always asked me as a kid for why I didn't take flowers to his grave. I never believed that he was dead. And therefore I go to that bar every night waiting for him to show up. If not for me, then for the love of alcohol, he should show up – he will show up," Rosita said standing in the centre of the kitchen, wiping the sweat rolling down her temple. She got back to her chopping.

She turned to me pointing the sharp steel knife and said, "Hope I have cleared all your doubts."

All these years I thought that she was a strong lady who was abreast with the world and was living contently with me. I had always thought of her as a young lady. But today I saw the fifty-year-old woman in her. I was looking at an old lady with grey hair. She was still hoping to find her lost husband who had been declared dead fifteen years ago.

All that was a little hard to understand, and lot harder to digest. Later that day, I narrated the whole story to Lucy, my girlfriend.

"She still thinks your dad is alive?" Lucy quirked, "Why don't you talk to her about this?"

"I don't think it would make any sense to talk to her. She has made up her mind. It has been going on for fifteen years now... or even longer," I replied.

"In that case, you should keep quiet and watch her," Lucy reverted. "Your mother is very vulnerable now. Her faith has not shattered over so many years. You just keep an eye on her and make sure she is okay. As you said, this is the one thing that has kept her going for all these years. It is possible that taking away this last glimmer of hope may leave her scarred for the rest of her life," she added.

I thought she was right so did nothing to disrupt my mother's routine. Like any other day, I went to bed and pretended to be asleep under the blanket until I heard Rosita leaving as usual. It went the same way for a couple of days. Eventually we all ended up accepting it as her choice. I had stopped paying much heed to the issue, for at least I knew that she was not visiting the bar to drink. She never found a need to discuss anything either.

I decided to focus on my work. I also thought it was time to settle down with Lucy. Lucy's dad, Mr Aldrin, was a real estate man and had a flourishing business. The number of rich people in Cortalim can be counted on your finger tips. Aldrin was one of those very few. Lucy had taken me to meet him to talk. Aldrin loved me, but the only condition he had was my job.

Cortalim did not have many opportunities. Besides, the whole of Goa had nothing much to offer me. I was currently working in a packaging firm in the city that also had offices in the United States. Lucy's dad decided it would do me good if we moved to the USA. It was almost all figured out, except for one big issue.

"Mom may not agree," I announced to Lucy sitting at the rocks by the beach.

"Why wouldn't she? She knows me, she likes me. She could not be less happy with us getting together," Lucy said.

"I am not talking about the marriage. She would not agree to leaving Cortalim. Her whole life has been here. Moreover, ever since she has told me about her daily bar trip, I doubt that I will be able to convince her to leave."

"But we need to talk to her. You never know, all this time she may be looking for a reason to quit her daily routine. This could be one of those decisions that may make her face reality."

"Let's see. Though I am sceptical." I sighed.

A week passed and I didn't spill a word to Rosita about my plans. I'd think of bringing it up every time at breakfast while she would rant about Cinderella's sickness or the leaking pipelines in the kitchen, and then back again at dinner time mostly between the same stories, but I got no way closer, until the day when she walked up to me in disquietude and said, "I found your dad."

I found your dad, she said.

"What are you saying?" I replied shocked.

"Yes, yes, yes you heard me right. I found him. I found Savio. I finally found him. All these days I was hunting for him with no leads. I almost decided to quit. But look, I am not wrong. I found your dad. My belief is intact; my hunt wasn't in vain," she shuddered.

"Mom, you are getting hysterical. Calm down and tell me the whole story. Are you sure it's dad?" I said as I made her sit on the couch. Rosita narrated what exactly happened with her the previous night.

I went to the bar and sat at the corner table. I pulled off my gloves from my hands and the stole from my face. Like every night, I was sipping my lime when this tall dark guy in shady glares walked up to me. At first I avoided making any conversation with him but then he took a chair at my table and said, "Not found what you have been looking for yet?" he grinned at me.

"What do you mean?" I interrogated.

He leered at me and said, "A beauteous woman like you, covered in black from head to toe visits the bar every night without a miss just to sip lime? You think just because you did not carry a sign board, no one will ever come to know?"

"What are you talking about? Come straight to the point," I said impatiently.

"I know where your husband is," he stared at me resting back on his chair.

He said he knows where Savio is and he could take me to meet him.

"Mom, I don't think this guy is genuine. There is no way he can make you meet dad. If dad was in Cortalim, where would he be possibly hiding from you all these years?" I said.

"He has asked me to show up tonight," she continued. "Finally things are moving and..."

"Mom, there is something I need to tell you."

"...all these years haven't been wasted," she continued to regurgitate her double decade journey when I had to intrude.

"We are moving to America."

Rosita pursed her lips and looked at me in astonishment. Her lips remained parted for a while as though she wanted to speak, but she didn't. She left the table and went inside the bedroom.

"I have got an offer from my company. They want me to shift to America. It will be good for us. I have things planned out. Please Mom, I need you to listen to me." I followed her.

I made voluble statements about our future and my career while Rosita kept folding the clothes and arranging them in the cupboard. I said every possible sentence that could have drawn her attention, but all I had was her oscillation with a pile of clothes.

"Do whatever you want. All that is important to me is finding my husband. I need to go see that person in the bar and then we can discuss the future later," Rosita finally said looking straight into my eyes.

After a spate of arguments, Rosita and I finally headed to the bar to wait for the man who was supposed to bring back my long lost father into our lives. An hour passed, but no one showed up. It was two in the morning. I yawned looking into my watch after every ten minutes. I tossed all the peanuts on the table, watched all the stories plotting on the tables around us, but no one showed up. The bar pulled down its shutter and we walked back home.

Rosita could not sleep that night. She didn't even change her clothes. I went off to work at noon while she was whipping the batter still in her blue-white-partially faded night gown. A little while later, a guy showed up at the door. It was the guy from the bar.

Rosita twitched at first but then he told her that he had not showed up the night before for he saw Rosita was accompanied by me. He didn't want me to come along to see Savio and that's why he waited at the other corner table for me to leave.

"Tonight, come alone. I will bring Savio along. And don't forget to get my reward. I need a big commission lady," the guy in shady glares said to Rosita. "Big day it is going to be lady... be ready!" he added.

Rosita was filled with hope again but she didn't tell me anything about the conversation with that guy. I assumed things were at bay and explained my entire plan of moving to America with her and Lucy after a small wedding in the town.

It was night and this time it appeared to me like Rosita had given up her hunt. The clock struck twelve but it did not seem that Rosita was going out. She finished cleaning the kitchen, locked the doors and switched off the light.

My assumptions put me to sleep, a tranquil sleep. The clock struck one and Rosita stoop up and sat on the bed. She sneaked out of the blanket.

It was six in the morning when I stretched my arms after a night of long, uninterrupted sleep, only to find all the gold was missing from the jewellery box. Some cash was missing from the wardrobe as well. Everything looked like it had been done twenty years ago when Rosita had eloped with Savio leaving Fransis behind. I had no inkling of what had taken place. I looked for Rosita in the room, in the bathroom and the kitchen, but she was nowhere to be found. Rosita's absence had only deepened the mystery.

I ran to the bar. I assumed she must have visited it again to look for the jerk baiting her. The only people on the road were the milk men, the newspaper guys, the wasted man sprawled down under a pole, and a retarded lady talking to herself while staring up at the sky. It was closed. All the nearby tea stalls and cigarette shops were shut as well. I looked around for a clue, a drunkard or mom anywhere close by when I heard a moaning goon lying outside the bar.

Dressed in a blue shirt, beige pants and brown jacket, the guy seemed to be singing in a weird language. I could smell the alcohol he had consumed overnight from his clothes. He had a grey beard and was unkempt. Marathi. He muttered something in Marathi while humming his song.

"Hey, did you see a lady in this bar last night?" I interrupted his singing. "Hey, hey, are you listening to me? I am looking for a lady. I was told she was in the bar last night. Have you seen her?" I persisted.

"Lady?" he slurred, "What lady?"

"A lady in a black coat. She comes here every night wearing a black coat, a stole and sits inside for hours. You have any idea?" I elaborated.

"No no, I don't know. Now buzz off, you fool, and let me enjoy my song. *Door halavi yasahi!*" he sassed.

I requested him once again but he kept humming his song, "*Mazhiya Pryiyala Preet Kalena...*"

I stepped away looking around but could see only a few stray dogs. I tried offering some money I had in my pocket to the drunkard. The lout stood up and snatched all of it saying, "I saw her. Saw her outside the bar. She stood here – near this pole, waiting for someone," he pointed at the one near the gates of the bar, "then..."

"Then, what happened? Tell me."

"I can't recall what happened after that. Give me some more money, I may think harder," he cadged me.

Handing him the remaining money in my pocket he told me that Rosita never entered the bar the previous night, unlike all the other nights. He had always noticed her entering the bar at around midnight and leaving at three every night. But the previous night, ten minutes after she arrived, a man walked up to her. She looked restless during her conversation with that man. Then she went with him.

"Where did she go?" I enquired.

"I assume they had a fag behind the bushes and then made out hard core," he riposted.

"*Snafu*! You better not dare to utter a word about her. She is my mother, you scoundrel. Mind your language," I cried as I reached for his collar.

"If she is your mother then how am I supposed to know where the hell the bitch is? You better take care of her." He snapped, parking himself back at his place.

"By the way, that man whom she was with is the janitor of the bone yard. He often comes around, covered all snazzy," he added.

I hardly waited for him to finish before I started running towards the cemetery. The road was rough and the straps of my slippers snapped before I reached the gates. I entered the cornered hut to look for the janitor. I came near the house and saw that though the doors were latched from the outside, a bulb inside was lit. I walked in calling for her. It had one bed room and a man was lying in it. The room was a mess. I shook the man to question him, but he seemed wasted. I stood up and turned around to walk out of the mess when I noticed Rosita's stole on the chair. Scrutinizing the room, it seemed apparent that some incident had taken place. The lamp shade was broken, broken pieces of things lay on the desk, the seemingly drunk man without a bottle of alcohol around him and Rosita's stole. Something was certainly up.

I did not know what to do. Where would I go looking for Rosita? What must have possibly happened the previous night? My head was hurting terribly. I walked out of the hut and sat down on the stairs assessing the numerous possibilities.

And only then, I saw her. It was Rosita sitting in front of me with legs crossed on Savio's gravestone. She was drinking; and this time, it wasn't lime. I walked up to her while she gulped the alcohol from the bottle and toasted it to Savio.

"Mom," I called her from behind. She turned back and smiled with the half empty bottle of whiskey in her hand. "What are you doing here?"

And then Rosita told me what had happened to her.

She had waited for the person with the shady glares to show up outside the bar and when he finally arrived he asked her if she has brought the reward. He said that Savio was waiting to see her and took her to the bone yard. Rosita followed his steps with the clutch in her hands, full of big cash and some jewels.

The man was quite intoxicated by then. He asked Rosita to wait for him and Savio in his hut when he hit her from behind and tried to rob her. Rosita shoved him back and hit him hard with her clutch when she dropped her stole on the chair. The guy was so wasted that he plopped down the floor and Rosita ran outside locking him in the hut.

"You know, all these years I learnt one lesson – to have faith; faith in my love that made me console myself every morning. Faith that Savio would come back. And funny story is that it took me a gash on that man's face and 2 pegs to unlearn the lesson," Rosita wept in elation.

"Faith is a bitch! You never know when it turns out to be a delusion. Now I know. And you know what, I am happy that finally I know," she added.

"Mom, are you alright?"

"I am great. Let's go to America," she raised her glass at me. "I am done here. I am done wallowing over things that don't exist and wasting my life. I think I need a real life now."

"You will. We all will. We are going to America and then there won't be any looking back," I promised her.

She raised her final toast, "To reality!" she said aloud and I joined her.

Rosita never went to the bar again. Lucy and I got married and the three of us moved to the States.

"Hey, where did you get this bottle from?" I asked

"I pilfered it from that man's hut after putting him to rest," she giggled.

It's Not A Love Story

A love story can begin anywhere: at the airport, a night club, a hospital, a college library, a college classroom, a college festival, under the college desks, at times even on the college desks and so on. But there is just a single place where they all get a closure – a bar.

This is not a story of how my love story ended or how I began a new one, but a story of a friendship that started…certainly not in the bar, but definitely because I was in a bar that day.

7 July 2011

It was Shyna's wedding day. She was on the podium wearing her fake smile and make-up in her blue lehenga. I had never seen her so happy before, nor so dressed up. The extra dark lip colour, the overlaid neck pieces, and above all, the copious amount of pink on her cheeks made her stand apart. The photographer clicked away – photographs that were soon to be uploaded on social networking sites as proof of the couple's happiness. Rest aside, she looked beautiful, more than ever.

I hung around for a while before the bride and groom headed for their photo session. I left thereafter.

I was returning from my ex's wedding. Do you know how it feels to be at your ex's wedding? The one day when she looks the most beautiful?

"You have no idea how it feels," I said half soaked in Chivas Regal, sitting in a bar with Mohit and Ravi.

"It's okay, Manas. Let it go. She has moved on. Anyway, I never liked her that much," Mohit replied.

"I know. But I don't know if I will ever find a girl like her again," I said.

"You will get even better ones, don't worry."

Mohit and I sat in the bar. I cribbed and he tried consoling me over every peg. Shyna and I had been in a relationship for almost five years and it took her barely an hour to put an end to it. I kept drinking the whole night, trying to overcome a relationship, while Ravi stayed glued to his phone trying to fix a relationship. He was convincing his girlfriend. About what I have no idea. They have been on phone for more than three hours now and the subjects of the arguments shifted from him coming late to her last birthday to my break up and finally to Ravi's gang, which included us.

"I have to leave guys," Ravi turned to us after hanging up his call.

"What happened?" Mohit asked.

"Shraddha is annoyed with me. She will kill me if I don't reach home in thirty minutes," Ravi said.

"But you said you will be staying back tonight. How can you ditch me?" Mohit said.

"I know, but just this time. I have no option left. I have to go. I am sorry, Manas," Ravi said turning to his jacket and the keys of his bike.

"But I cannot stay, you know that. It's *the* night," Mohit said to Ravi.

"It's okay, guys. You can leave. I am fine. Don't worry about me," I said.

"No, let me drop you home. You are too wasted to drive back home," Mohit said, lifting my arms to his shoulders.

"What is tonight?" I questioned Mohit.

"Tanya and I are finally making a move. Now we are not as lucky as you guys to have the entire apartment to ourselves. After so long we have..." Mohit told me about his plans for the night while Shyna's face kept flashing in front of me.

I still remembered the first time when we had made love in my apartment. I remembered her eyes, the most beautiful thing in the world; confused eyes filled with naïveté. Her hands soft like that of a baby's and the cute dimple on her chin. Her body was like a bottle of wine to me – it just felt better every time I touched it. I pulled open the knot of her blouse from the back and moved my hands on her body. It was silk. It was the night of the Garba festival when I had been to Ahmedabad to see her while she was interning in a law firm. We had returned from the dance and got drunk as hell. I held her tight and we laid ourselves on the floor with our lips melting into each other's.

My pleasant memories were suddenly interrupted,

"One thousand rupees I said, or you'll be in trouble," a goon of a traffic police constable was having a dialogue with Mohit. "No drinking and driving allowed, sir. I cannot let you pass," he added.

Mohit handed him a five hundred rupee note and tried to settle the matter. All I remember was the Marathi-speaking constable with his little moustache over red lips stained with tobacco. Mohit drove me home and put me to sleep.

The next morning I woke up after the sun had passed the prime meridian. Whether one is getting into a relationship or breaking out of it, some things continue to remain unchanged like being in the bed for most part of the day. I remained in bed till eight in the evening for there seemed nothing worthy to wake for. In my apartment, which had four occupants, I was by myself with Fraddy. Fraddy was Farhan, who was physically present with us but mentally in his own world most of the time. He had been an engineering student for the past eight years and was still in his final year. All Fraddy did the whole day was smoke his marijuana and play the never-ending playlist of EDM tracks in his ipod.

Usually I hardly spoke to Fraddy, but this was no usual day. It was a day when any company was good company.

We doped awaiting the remaining two members to come in and feed us some real food. At midnight we left for the bar and got drunk good.

"You know what, it's not that bad hanging out with you. All these days I thought you found me quite pesky," I said to Fraddy taking a sip from my peg.

"Actually, I found your girlfriend very pesky. Now that you two have separated, it's good to have you around, brother. Cheers!" said Fraddy.

We left the bar in a few hours on my bike when I was pulled aside by the same constable who had caught us the previous night.

"A thousand rupee fine or..." he said handing me a receipt, "Aren't you the same guys from last night? You are back?"

"You might have to adjust a little bit, *bhau*, it's a matter of love," I responded pulling out a five hundred rupee note from my wallet and said, "You will be seeing a lot of me."

My cell phone bleeped as it received a notification on Facebook that read, 'Shyna Watwe is married to Tejas Mahajan'.

"The news on Facebook has started travelling faster than light. They aren't yet done with their first night after marriage and it's on their timeline already," I said taking the stand up and starting the engine. And though I just mentioned that it's about love, what's coming ahead is *not a love story!*

After that night, every night I would cross the same way while returning from the bar – half-soaked in alcohol – and every night was intercepted by the same constable. He would chastise me and would put his receipt back along with the five hundred rupee note in his hands. Some days I would go along with a friend, the other days on my own. He had eventually started to recognize my motor bike from a distance and would stand ready to give me a ticket. It went on for exactly eight nights till one night finally I stopped by the square.

I parked my bike and staggered towards him and bent my head to read his badge, "Anand Satpute," I slurred. "Don't you want to charge me a fine tonight?"

Satpute looked at me and said, "My wife is in love with you."

I looked at him in astonishment and said, "What?"

"And so are my kids. They have been wondering who is this person filling my pocket with five hundred rupees every day," he said.

"Good for you. Don't you want another one tonight?"

"Why do you drink and drive every night? Are you Ambani's son?"

"You never know. I may be." I burped.

"Huh! Ambani. Have you ever looked yourself in the mirror?" he turned away grinning at my looks, "but, seriously, why do you drink so much? Is there some problem? Girl issue... oh! Yes, I remember you said something about love. So some girl broke your heart?"

I chuckled tipsy, "We are the people of the smart phone generation. We don't have heart breaks, we just change our model," I said reaching for my wallet.

"Let it be," he intruded, "Go away and you better not show me your face again".

"That, I cannot promise, Mr Satpute," I put my wallet back and rode away.

It is advisable that to overcome a break up one must get engaged to some*thing* and not some*one*. I definitely had got the most intoxicating thing to engage me and that had given me a someone to engage with – a traffic constable.

Every other night following that I would stop by the square, have a talk with Satpute, bug him for a while, listen to a lecture from him and then leap on my bike and zoom off.

"Satpute!" I saluted him in the middle of the street.

"Not again. Get a job, you spoilt brat. If your dad has too much cash, give it to me instead," Satpute said.

"I got a whiff of your intentions a long time back. That's why you intercept me every night here," I jigged at him.

"Why do you have to drink so much? You don't even want the girl anymore. What's the point?"

"Who said I don't want her anymore? Of course I do," I yelled standing under the lamp post.

"Then, why don't you tell her? You believe your alcoholism will convey your message to her, you son of Devdas?"

"Umm..." I gestured to him to come closer so that I could reach his ears and whispered, "She's married now."

"Married. Oh! So you are truly a son of Devdas!"

"But, I wish..."

I giggled. And I giggled hard, rolling down the ground. Then getting back on my feet, I threw up.

"But, I just wish she had talked to her parents about us. She never even told me. One night she was with me and the next morning she was engaged. And in between, all I got was, 'It's okay Manas, anyway my parents would have never agreed to our relationship'. How did she know it already? She should have taken courage to talk to them first. Of course, I understand she wanted to stay in a big city," I said and sat down.

"Why didn't you talk to her parents? I would have stormed to her place, if I were you," Satpute said sitting down beside me.

"My grandma has cancer... last stage. No one has time for my love story at this moment. "

"I think, somewhere, you knew it."

"Knew what?"

"That she was going to leave you. And you were quite ready to let her go, but you were not quite ready to be left alone," Satpute said.

"You think so?"

"I know so. And even you know so. You just can't live with the fact that she is happy and settled with someone who is not you and you have no one with you."

I shrugged saying, "Maybe. But I also wish... she was here. I wish..."

I woke up groggy and dishevelled that morning and the room looked exactly the way it had looked when Shyna and I used to wake up in the mornings following every party night. The common perception is that on an average, boys drink more than girls do. But few girls might make you alter your perception. She was a big tank. And after getting drunk she would be turned on. We would get wasted all night and the night would end with

Shyna hurling in the middle of the street and me taking care of the car, and then her of course.

Satpute drove me back home and helped me walk through the corridor. I am a bit foggy on details of that night but Fraddy narrated the entire scene the next morning.

"He enquired about the MH police street hurdle," Fraddy said.

"Jesus Christ! It slipped from my head. What did you say?" I asked Fraddy.

"What did I say? Fed him with your mother's hand-made laddoos over tea. Thank god she makes such yummy sweets. It saved the day."

A Maharashtra Police street hurdle is one of those rectangular long yellow stands which we often notice on the roads slowing the cars down. It was one of those nights where none of us were in our senses. We had picked one up and brought it home. Unfortunately, Maharashtra Police was soaked under our white and blue underwear drying on it when Satpute had a rendezvous with it.

We were taken aback by the fact that he had overlooked the street hurdle of Maharashtra Police in our hall.

I had no idea where my life was going and I had no idea why meeting Satpute on the way had become a habit. I was in no way trying to get into his pants. I was still pretty much straight. The idea of being reprimanded by him every day was comforting.

"I heard you dropped me back home last night," I said heading towards Satpute in the centre of Parel the next night.

"That would be a thousand bucks and five hundred bucks more for breaking my arm under your shoulder last night."

"Sorry I can't give you anything," I said smirking at him. "I am not drunk tonight and I am sorry for last night," I added returning to my bike.

"Are you fine?" Satpute intervened.

"I am trying," I said turning back to him. "Have you ever been in this situation?"

"What situation?"

"A mushy love story where everything sounds perfect, but at the end it is just a big mess."

"I practically face this situation every day at home. I thought that life would be perfect...having a wife and a kid. And being with your own family is all you need to be happy. But when I look back I wonder if I really needed it. I had been a lot better and stress free without the daily bickering."

We chuckled at each other and we chuckled till we were in the bar raising a toast at each other's failures.

"Actually, I think it's only for the better. She wants different things; I want different things. We would have never worked together. So, in a way, it has happened for some good," I said twirling the ice in my glass.

"What did she want?"

"She always wanted to stay here, in Mumbai. I, on the other hand, am a small town boy. She would have never lived with me there. And even if I had got her along through all the emotional drama and tantrums, neither of us would have been happy. I have a joint family; she was born and brought up in a boarding school. To me, my family is the most important – my strength, my weakness, my life support. How could she have been happy? Besides, I don't think it was easy being with her."

"I know, girls get over-demanding at times and our pockets start to shrink, maintaining their nail paint bills!"

"Yes. And even then she was always complaining. 'You never give me time, you never support me against my friends, and you never behave like Aarti's boyfriend.' I mean seriously! Aarti's boyfriend was a pimp. Does Aarti even know about it?"

"Never mind, the brighter part is that it's over. Cheers to that."

"Imagine the worst thing that we fought about? One of my friends saying 'Let it go' while I was in a fight with Shyna and she by mistake read that message. Now the fact that I didn't reply to my friend is what we fought over for nearly four hours. Could it be worse?" I said asking for another round of drinks for both of us and then another.

That night Satpute had a glimpse of his never-ending enigma of a happy life when he was dropped home by me at six in the morning. For one night, the poor guy forgot that he had a wife waiting for him back home.

Reasonably or unreasonably, I had found someone to open up to and it was amazing. He didn't know me, neither did he know Shyna. The chances of him throwing the regular confab at me of pretending to dislike her, when he was one of the many trying to woo her, were a lot less. But that was not the only reason to be around him. After a long while I had found someone more sensible than me to talk to, especially at the time when I needed to the most.

I started drinking to forget Shyna. Eventually, she merely became a subject of our conversation as we drank together. Parel's streets had started to see more of me than its bars.

A couple of days later I visited him at the same pole, but not while returning from the bar. A couple of constables stood there awaiting the next victim. I preened for Satpute, as I could not find him there. I questioned the constables and I learned that Satpute was in the hospital. I took the details and rushed to the hospital to check on him.

I found him sitting in the waiting area in his uniform. He was sweating and there was a frown on his forehead. I had never seen him so disturbed before. What possibly could have gone wrong to reduce a guy like Anand Satpute to this state?

"She was perfect until yesterday. Her hands were twitching a little, but we didn't pay much heed. Today, her left hand stopped moving. They have diagnosed tuberculosis in her spine. She must be operated upon immediately or she might not survive it. I have no clue where to arrange such a big amount of money from," Satpute told me.

"Don't worry brother. *Me Marathi manusach, Marathi mansachi madad karu shakto,*" I consoled him.

It was time for me to use my rich dad connections. Shyna's husband was the grandson of the MLA in Mumbai. This was one way to repay the money for all her four shots of tequila, two bottles of beer and one peg of whiskey that she would always end throwing up.

The doctors were asked to start the treatment right away and Anand breathed easy.

"I am short of words to thank you. You have no idea how grateful I am to you at this moment," Satpute said in a choked voice. "Let me make you a drink tonight."

"It's okay. I think you should be with your wife tonight. I will see you soon," I said taking my leave.

"Manas," I turned back when he called my name, "It was for the best that you didn't marry Shyna."

"Good for you – good for me," I said and turned back.

And it was then that a middle-aged man finally made me get over my ex and rather celebrate it, for my loss has been everybody's gain; even my own today.

I found a friend 2 peg ke baad when I lost my love.

Epilogue

2010, Kolkata

Every night a lady preened herself in the mirror under the light of an oil lamp in a house where she resided all alone. She made herself a stiff peg of desi alcohol and drank a mouthful followed by another peg of the same. She sipped her way through the second peg while she looked at herself in the mirror. Holding her eyeliner in one hand darkening the waterlines of her eyes, she let out a murmur of appreciation for every sip of her drink. 2 pegs ke baad she got on her feet and started to do Kathak dance, singing a poem in the name of Lord Radhe-Krishna. The whole night she danced, forgetting everything around her in remembrance of God, and offering her beauty and art through her hands, face, eyes, voice, feet and ornaments.

Few years back

It was raining outside at seven o'clock in the morning. Laxmi woke up with the sound of the raindrops on her roof. She put a leg out of her bed and collapsed. She lifted herself up and forced herself to stand up. She stood up and collapsed again. She collapsed three times that morning until she stopped feeling her feet. Laxmi was in a paralysis: sleep paralysis.

2012, The University of Nottingham, UK

"The best revenge is massive success." Born and raised with the same belief in Scotland, my entire life was a reflection of taking revenge. My parents had a failed marriage – the effect of which I keep taking out on my relationships. My bad relationships have made me take revenge over the busty rats running with me to win the race – at work and in the college – and to keep myself going, I keep reminding myself of the same theorem repeatedly.

I was a student at Nottingham University, and was doing my Master's in journalism to get back at my last break-up. I had been left at the altar on the day of my wedding.

I am Lisa and this story isn't about me.

With every semester, we were supposed to submit a documentary which went to the jury and the best ones got screened in the international film festival. By the year 2012, students of Nottingham were living in the era of the three R's – Racism-Riots-Rifles, and one of the subjects of interest was terrorism. However, documenting ISIS was beheading oneself in advance.

"India!" a bunch of half-wasted idiots sitting in the bar shouted in unison. "Why are you going to India? If there has to be a documentary, it could be anywhere around here in Europe itself," Gayale, one of the exchange students from Argentina added.

"Sure, I mean there are enough stories around us, in fact you wait for an hour and you may pull out a good number of stories from this very spot," jibbed Soma who was an Indian of Bengali descent.

"I agree, but I have completed my research," I answered.

"See, that's the benefit of doing a documentary in a bar, you don't need a research," Soma jibbed again.

"Plus, it's cost effective. All you need to do is focus on those bimbos sitting in the corner and wait for the right time. The story is right there. Epilogue: Alcohol has been playing a very important role in our lives and as a journalist I highly encourage it as a noteworthy tool to expose secrets," said Merranda hitting the last shot on the table.

We all chuckled holding on to a few more shots.

"America and Australia were far reaching provinces in the eyes of a financer, plus sex would be too profound to be brought under documentation and yet less appreciated by our class of audience. Arabic countries are too rich to be positive about – all they have got is execution. The rest of Europe has nothing we want to know about anymore. Japan is too out of reach, and if technology was one of the things that we are talking about, which we are not, I would rather head to China. But right now it's India. Why you ask – cheap on production, easy on laws, people are really interested to tell their stories and the best part: you go there looking for one story and you come back with ten," I said smirking.

"Great, so what are you looking for?" asked Edwin who was another descendant from the English bay like me.

"Not sure yet, but I am interested to cover the transgender section there," I replied.

"Why transgender? I mean, when there is poverty, polygamy, polyandry even in the present day. Dowry, child marriage, caste system, rape – those seem to be the hot topics," Edwin said.

I intruded him, "Rape has already been covered in depth during recent times."

"The point is why would you choose only the transgender section as a subject?" he asked.

"Yes, and if you really want that, better plan a trip to Thailand and have a holiday interviewing shemales instead of panting in the slums of India," Soma rejoined.

"True that. I will think it over again. But the more the poverty, the better the chances for international films," I stated.

The next day, I went across all the transgender documentation from India. I came across links which had stories of their bitterness and the social stigma against them. While looking up on the internet, I stumbled on an interesting festival that transgender people from South India celebrate – Koovagam.

"Just like Good Friday is to us and Muharram to the Islamic, the people of the transgender community cry in the name of Prince Aravan, who died the very next day of being wedded to one of the Hindu gods," I explained at the table of the bar while we all caught up the next evening for drinks. "The god had transpired as a woman just to marry him, even though he was aware that he would die the very next day."

"Wow! I have never heard of it. I think you must go and attend it," Gayale said helping himself to a chicken wing.

"He is right. But when is this festival happening?" asked Merranda.

"Luckily, next week," I smiled.

"That's great. I am taking a flight home the same time. In fact, we can travel to India together," Soma said excitedly.

"Really! That will really be great. So you finally got some time off from your office?" I queried. Soma had a long standing issue with her boss who would not allow her to take a trip home to her own sister's wedding.

"I got fired," she said, "and I also quit, so fair enough!" Soma added sipping her Jamtini slowly unlike other days when she would gulp it down jittered with her boss. "Why don't you come to Kolkata with me?" she then tossed.

"Kolkata? What's there?" I enquired.

"The greatest brothel in India – Sonagachi."

"But I am not looking for sex workers, but people from the transgender community."

"It's kind of the same there. You will find it all there. Where exactly do you plan to go for this festival?" Soma asked.

"Tamil Nadu – some district named Villu-puram," I said.

"Great! Come and stay at my place for two days. I will show you around Kolkata and if you want, we can even go to hunt for some content for your documentary and then you can fly to Villupuram," Soma said looking at me.

The next week Soma and I were on a flight to India along with my crew. Our first stop was in Mumbai from where we were supposed to change a flight. An agent from Tamil Nadu was helping me with my stay and finding the right people for my story. This could be one of my best works and if all went well, this would be the one revenge turning sweet at me. I had my fingers crossed for the week that was to come.

We arrived at the Mumbai airport after the fourteen-hour-long flight. Two hours later, we were in Kolkata.

This story isn't about Kolkata.

We had landed in the 'City of Joy'. The little I had known about Kolkata was the famous *Durga puja* and its extravagant literary and artistic class that would even beacon Europeans to take a relook at themselves. The city smelled sometimes like a fish and at other times like a bigger fish. We settled down at Soma's place for the night.

The next morning I was taken to the congested lanes of Shobhabazar that were filled with water choking the drains. A drainage line passed from between the narrow yard dividing the row houses on each side. Among the shades of green and blue painted kaccha houses, we were introduced to a group of transgender people or eunuchs residing there.

It was interesting to discover that here eunuchs were synonymous to sex workers. Talking with them I managed to get quite a few details about their lives. Begging, dancing and prostitution are their major ways of making a living. They would clap around the shops and other public places like traffic signals and railway stations to indulge in something of a cross between begging and extortion. Where some would pay them willingly, others did that grudgingly.

I got to talk to a couple of them. One of them was an HIV patient who had been living in the area for more than two decades after her castration and had been making a living by selling her body. But lately, after she discovered her illness, she continued doing the same only for a good amount and made sure her clients used condoms.

One thing common to all the people I talked to was the injustice done to them by society. Yet their faith in God was such that would never unhinge.

I took random shots of them. Of them telling their stories, playing with their hair, their rants against the society and their families, and the one common prayer that I got from all of them: "I wish in my next life God makes me either a man or a woman; not a mixture of the two."

I was perturbed after spending an hour with them. Living with what you have been given by nature against the acceptance of the society was a baptism on fire. But they would never give up believing in God. Regular rituals were conducted to thank God and please all the deities for the life given to them and to others around them.

I was invited to watch the grand Durga Puja to take place later in the evening and the celebrations following them. I stayed back with one of my team members and asked Soma to leave. My flight to Villupuram was scheduled for the next day and I was hoping to get some content that had never been captured by National Geographic or the BBC.

At the puja, one of the eunuchs who was of a higher designation would dance in the name of God and would eventually give up as she transformed to a possessed being, which was believed to be the coming of Goddess Durga into one's body. There was no explanation for the inebriate dancing, the gulping of camphor and the goddess residing in the body of the eunuch, but to the people around me, it was as good as facing the goddess herself.

After the regular singing and dancing, they would drink for fun and continue with the celebrations. People around them would gather to take part in the same and it carried on till midnight.

Watching them boozing and enjoying themselves was something interesting, but not interesting enough for me to stay back and keep the camera rolling.

While I had gathered a good number of tapes to add to my documentation, I decided to make a move from their locality. Walking back from the lanes of Shobhabazar, I noticed that the market seemed to have transformed to an altogether different place at night. I walked past the gaudily dressed ladies luring men on the streets for the night.

My attention was drawn to the window of a room. A poem sung from the inside could be heard with notes of classical music in between. I peered into it from the little divide of its entrance. An oil lamp was all that illuminated the floor. Only then, I heard the fall of a foot beneath the jangle of ghungroos. A lady was dancing, dressed in a blue sari, glitter everywhere on her body, thick eyeliner around her eyes and a big red spot on her forehead – like an ideal Indian classical dancer.

Her look was mesmerizing and so was her dance. I stood on the door watching her dance with the rhythm of the song which was in the praise of Lord Krishna. With every change in action, the agility of her footwork increased along with the flamboyance of her expressions. The room seemed to be spangled by the glint of her face. Her eyes gave away a million emotions – they had love, they had joy, they had rage, and they pleaded for mercy while she threw herself on the floor.

I could feel the walls of the room vibrating around me as her performance proceeded. Her feet got faster and my attention got deeper. She went around her axis for about a minute and then collapsed on the floor. I waited for her to get up, but she fell unconscious. The room was sedated. There was absolute silence inside. I stepped in to wake her up. I turned her towards me while she was drenched in sweat and smelled nothing less than a bottle of wine. Yes – she looked equally sedating herself, but it occurred to me that she was quite drunk.

I called her a few times before she responded exaltedly in a heavy voice. She was an extremely beautiful lady with big eyes. Her face was lit by the light of the lamp in the room and the grace of her dance had made me forget the rest of my day in the city. She murmured something in Bengali in a loud voice which scared me and I moved away from her. It wasn't like a woman's. I stepped back baffled by her tone when it struck me that she was probably a eunuch.

The next morning I was supposed to catch my flight to Villupuram. The entire night had me pondering over the most interesting thing I had ever come across. I got ready to leave for the airport. My flight was in five hours when I realized my phone was missing. I must have dropped it the previous night in that dancer's room, I thought. I confirmed my boarding time and took a cab back to Shobhabazar.

The doors were open. I barged into the house hoping to find someone. It was all quiet inside. I looked around for my phone when I was set back by a six feet tall glittering image of a Hindu god and goddess.

"I guess you are here to take you phone," a voice took me away from the image. It was the dancer from last night.

"I am sorry, I could not find anyone," I said trembling.

"Here it is," she handed me my phone. "I suppose you were here last night?" she interrogated.

"Yes, I was passing by when I saw you dancing and it caught my attention right away. You dance exquisitely," I replied.

"I guess I was born to be a dancer. I assume you must be a reporter all the way to get a story on poverty, sex workers or transgender issues, right?"

"Transgender," I accorded.

"So, did you get a story?"

"Not quite. It is the same old story of the stigma around them that is being covered since ages, nothing new. The dark past, the trade of their body for their livelihood, the NGOs leading them into sex education and the never-ending fight with the society documented by hundreds in the past."

"What else do you want? You have got all the emotional spice to take away the accolades of the jury."

I chuckled at her statement, "Looks like you know quite a lot about journalism."

"Not too much. But I believe we are all looking for that certain spice in our lives. When you are a man you try finding it in a woman and vice-a-versa."

"And what about eunuchs, what do they look for?"

"They don't have to. They are born with it. At first it's their sex and later it is sex they desire to attract others towards them – and when all is done, they come back to the worry that everyone else irrespective of their sex ends up with: who will be with me in my last days?"

I did not know how to respond to her argument as more than being convinced, I was taken aback by the truth of life spilled in front of me in two sentences.

"What do you think...?" she asked me as she watered the plants in her corridor.

"Lisa and I couldn't agree more," I replied introducing myself.

"I am Laxmi," she retorted.

"Well, I wonder if your spice is dancing"

"Dancing is not my spice; it is rather my tool to add the spice. For someone it would be their assets or to most in my line, the not having of those assets would be the one."

"I do not understand you. You dance dressing up like an Indian classical dancer and dance in an empty room appreciating yourself...but to lure whom?" I turned to Laxmi.

"Him," she said turning back and pointing at the six feet image of Lord Krishna in front of her, "to my Krishna," she added.

◆

"I was born and raised differently. For most parents, having a boy is an issue but they were lucky to have me as a boy. However, my body grew differently as I grew older. I developed a body and a soul of a girl. I was only fourteen when I came here and have never looked back ever since," Laxmi said handing me a cup of tea and settling down in a corner sipping from her's.

"As a human being, I was always looking for happiness and found them in things that were always out of my reach. When I was a kid, my greatest question was my own sex and detesting it all, I wished to be at either end of the race: a man or a woman. As I grew older I accepted my body and its changes but the greater quest was to find someone who would appreciate it in the same way. I was looking for happiness in the opposite sex. To attain that, I ended up reaching my guru's feet to get castrated. Looking up to my deities I was castrated under no injection or pills, bleeding away, hoping the blood to take away all the pain in me.

"But pain is never rewarded; it is the creation of our own imagination. I felt more powerful after being castrated and more like a woman now, but the quest was not over. It had only begun there.

"As a young lady I highly appreciated my body. I looked pretty and I would preen at the mirror for hours feeling the woman within me. I loved my hair, my breasts, my eyes and my waist. I would admire my body all the time, would play with my hair and feel my breasts. The confidence in my beauty made me happy. I stood outside in the corridor to look at the guys passing by. They looked back at me exchanging gestures of sycophancy.

"As a kid I was made to do little household work and would be served in return. Now I was a lady and a beautiful one at that. I was expected to go and earn. Half the share of my earnings went to my guru, and from him, to his guru, and so on. The remaining half was spent by me on vanity. I loved to dress up and dance. I would go dancing and singing with my friends and other troop members to earn money.

"The ghungroos found their way right from there. I started saving my money from the little that I earned and learnt classical dance after work. Dance gave me happiness. It was the one thing that made me forget my body; while dancing it was me who had to play both male and female in one body. It was the expression of who I was and the way I felt being it.

"But when the ghungroos were pulled off, I was reminded of the reality and the emptiness it held. It was no more the body that was looking for acceptance, but my heart instead. It desired love. Love of a person of the opposite sex. Men would look at me, get impressed and flirt with me, but the moment they would learn the truth about me, the only thing they'd come down to was my body.

"The one thing that I stopped chasing was right ahead of me. Now they needed my body; the one thing that they once rejected.

"So I slept for love. And I slept again and then again until love chose to settle down as one night pleasure. Before I knew it, I was sleeping for pleasure. I had sex for money and soon I started enjoying it.

"Customers would come and have a few drinks with me, would talk to me about the early wrangle with their wives or bosses or take me to bed. Some came in for they had had two or more kids and did not find their wives interesting anymore, some liked it with a different person and to do things differently, while some would barely do anything and instead just talk about their bad days at work or with their wives.

"That was when I found the answer to one of my quests – the answer to my own sex.

"What happiness did they get living on one edge of the race. Men came to me for pleasure, cursing their women who were being cheated on by their own men.

"Some were willing to date me but would change their minds the moment their feet touched the ground outside the bed. Even the ones with longer foreplay and with more intense kisses than ever, failed to arouse me any longer. After a few years of selling myself to make a living, I looked for a way to turn it back. It was all about having a few drinks, spreading my legs and moaning to fake an orgasm.

"When sex could not turn you on, what possibly could.

"Lying under a random guy who does not even know your name, I used to think – is that all I was born for? Is life to me just about drinking-having sex-sleeping? What is the motive of my life?

"My life was summarized into singing-dancing-eating-sleeping. I felt worse than an animal; a cow who would give more than I do as a livestock, work harder in the farm than I do and serve the leather industry even after it expires; a dog, whose flesh would feed hungry scavengers; a lizard, who would do as much as I do but be the food to a snake to maintain the life cycle.

"I kept wondering what good I was doing and how I was any better than any of those. I had no role in the society, not even as entertainment.

"Then I tied these ghungroos around my ankles and started dancing. I felt I had finally found what I had been looking for. I started teaching dance in the day and I would dance with my friends in the night.

"I felt content, more than I would feel after a climax. I was doing at least some good. I was making some difference to someone. I was finally of good use to someone."

There was a knock on the door. Laxmi's students had arrived. They tied their ankle-bells around and Laxmi began singing her song which she called a *kavit* in dancing terminology. Her students were young girls learning to express their love for God through dancing.

Laxmi was right; dancing made her truly contented. I took a look at my watch and I had three hours to catch the flight to cover my story, but I was wondering whether I had already found one.

I waited for her class to get over. The girls offered their prayers to the ground and touched Laxmi's feet before they left.

"So, that was about teaching dance. What about last night? And what about Lord Krishna?" I asked Laxmi.

"Have you heard the story of Prince Aravan?" she asked me.

"Of course, and that is the reason why I have been planning to visit Tamil Nadu."

"When no princess got ready to marry the prince, knowing that he would die the very next day, it was Lord Krishna who took the form of a princess and rescued his devotee by marrying him. There lies a part of Krishna in all of us. We all are finding the remaining half. Why don't we find the form of Krishna – bliss – in him itself," Laxmi said leaving me mystified by her statement.

"It was raining outside at seven o'clock in the morning. I woke up with the sound of the raindrops on my roof. I put a leg out of my bed and collapsed. I forced myself to stand up. I stood up and collapsed again. I collapsed three times that morning until I stopped feeling my feet. I was in a paralysis: sleep paralysis.

"For months I was bedridden and often thought what wrong I must have done that this had happened to me. I gave up sex; I gave up demanding for justice. I accepted my destiny in his will, yet I wondered why this had happened to me. I lay on the bed weeping and praying for help.

"It was then that I started drinking. It was the only way to escape the pain. The number of pegs increased with time, but its effect had reduced. When my friends would drink along with me, we celebrated. They danced for me and I enjoyed watching them. On other days I would make myself 2 pegs to put myself to sleep, to forget the pain and the world around me.

"People from NGOs would come to help, but I had given away all hope. Until I discovered myself outside my body. I gave myself to Krishna. After all, it was Krishna who showed acceptance towards Aravan when no one else did.

"My faith helped me recover.

"I dance every morning to make others happy and I dance again in the night to make my Lord happy. I drink to forget the world around me, because the world inside of me is much prettier and it comes up only once the rest of the world fades away. The world around us has problems – problems that would allure us towards them and gives us pleasure. The pleasure of earning money, having kids, finding true love, having sex – the list is endless. But once I drink to forget them, all that stands in front of me is Krishna, and when I dance for my Krishna, I get the ultimate pleasure. It's beyond anything else and at least I know that it will not reduce its effect with time; would only become more sublime," Laxmi said looking at the image of Lord Krishna with love.

Few days later
The University of Nottingham, UK

It was the day of my presentation and I had put together the most beautiful collection of thoughts I have ever experienced. I stood at the lectern when the first slide of my presentation with Laxmi's picture on it was displayed.

"Good evening respected jury members, professors and dear audience. Last week I made a visit to Kolkata, which is a city in east India and had an encounter with a couple of transgender people, also known as eunuchs or *hijrahs*," I pitched the prologue, "...but this story isn't about eunuchs..." I added.

There was a hiss in the audience when I continued, "...It's about finding happiness."

Euphobia

There are a lot of ways for me to begin a story. Sometimes I begin by the stuff that leads to the main story, the other times I jump right into the climax and then slowly go back to the past. But for this story, I have no shrewd way to begin. Mostly because I still don't know if it was a hallucination, I mean just a hallucination, or was there more to it. One big reason that the story came about, to be was my insobriety. Though it still feels like just another dream to me.

PS: It was not a dream!

Like I said, I have no smart way to commence, but let's start with it anyway. I, Akshay Rudhra, Software Engineer, was working with an IT firm in Chennai and believe me, what it takes to be an IT professional in a leading multinational is beyond sweat and blood, at times even your senses.

It was a dull Sunday afternoon. On most Sundays I would go to play billiards with friends, or would be at my girlfriend's apartment nursing the hangover from the previous night. But sadly, this time the season was all dry. Mainly because I had no girlfriend, and all my friends were either busy with dates, or back home to celebrate Diwali with family, or married. So I was all by myself this time. Despite that, surprisingly, it wasn't going that bad. My servant Mutthu had taken a day off from work and I was all alone at my place. I lay the whole afternoon in my boxers, eating pop corn, sipping beer and watching horror movies.

There was no food in the kitchen, so I made myself a cheese omelette and guzzled it down with beer. The weather was not too clement and I was happy to be at home. I was four bottles of beer down when I was done watching the fourth part of *Grudge*. I moved towards the kitchen to get some more popcorn and another round of beer when I heard some clattering outside.

I looked outside: it was a window banging against the wall. It was quite dark as I leaned out to shut the window. I drew in the panes and headed back to my couch.

It was midnight when I finished my marathon movie session. The movie had the one-eyed ghost moaning towards her target, with half her face covered by her hair. Shoot! That was the end of the tale.

I was so tired and high that I switched off the television and snuggled inside my blanket. In the middle of the night, a sound from my bedroom woke me up. It was something like the shattering of glass. I was too drowned in beer to get up to check the cause of the sound. Before I could fall asleep, I heard another cracking sound. I got out of my quilt drowsily, with my eyes half shut, and dragged myself to the bedroom. There were some pieces of broken glass with some of my stationery lying on the floor. I looked at the window banging beside the study table and closed it shut. I looked across the hall and everything seemed to be in place.

I stood there wondering for a while when there was a knock on my window behind my couch. It was two in the morning and storming outside. My friends were out of town, and I could not think of anyone who could possibly be there at that hour. The water ran down the panes of the window from outside and all I could see was a hand hitting against them.

I went blank for a second. I shouted to ask the person his identity, but there was no reply.

Suddenly, it was silent. The knocking on the window stopped. I ran my eyes on the windows end-to-end, but could see nothing.

I gathered it must have been the beer playing cheap tricks on my mind and so I went back to cuddle my pillow. I cleared the mess on my couch including my empty beer bottles. Only then I noticed some blood on it. It was from my fingers. I must have got a cut from the glass pieces back in the room. I looked for the wound but found none. The next second I realized that I wasn't even bleeding and the blood on my fingers what not really mine. I was clueless of where it had come from and only then I heard another knock on my door.

Someone banged it rough.

"Who...who's there?" I asked, but there came no answer. I though it must be some sort of a prank, so I went close to the door to look through the peep hole. There was a really old man standing there. He seemed to be struggling to stand still. His sagging face gave me a furious look.

"Open the door," the old man cried as he looked back at me from the hole.

I was numb with shock. He kept knocking at the door for a while.

"Who are you? What do you want?" I asked loudly.

"My wife," he said.

"Your wife?" I muttered to myself. "Your wife is not here. No wives are here. You are at the wrong place, sir. I live here alone. Please stop banging the door and go back home," I shouted and went back to my couch.

The knocking had stopped. But not a minute later, he started again. He knocked slowly but loudly.

"Sir, please go back. There is no one here."

"What did you do to her? She got hurt; she must be bleeding. Open the door, I want to see my wife," he yelled from outside.

I was a bit daunted listening to him and also worried for he was a guy looking for his wife at two o'clock in the morning.

He stood there knocking for another hour, all the while babbling about his injured wife. I wanted to help him and stop the disturbance, so I decided to call the police. I reached for my phone to make the call, but found that the battery was completely discharged. I looked for the charger and remembered that it was on my study table in my room. I ran inside the room to get the charger. The lights in the room were off and it was dark except for the light streaming in from the hallway. I looked down and started scrolling for the phone number when something suddenly stopped me. I raised my eyes above my cell phone and turned towards my right. It was absolute dark on the other side of the room.

I tried to scream and tried making some kind of sound but choked. I wanted to scream and call for help, but I couldn't shout. The lightening outside lit up the easy chair moving in front of me on the other side of the room and there was a lady sitting on it. The phone slipped from my hand and I ran out of the room.

She was bleeding. She was bleeding from her right arm and down her clothes. She had her eyes wide open, staring at me. She would not blink even once. I wondered if she was even alive. My voice was choked and before I could think, I latched the door from outside.

The knocking on the door could be heard no more.

My mind was flooded with thoughts. How long had the lady been here? When did she come in and from where had she entered the house? I had been home the whole day? And how come she was bleeding?

It was possible that she was still alive. But I had no guts to check in on her. I swallowed hard and before I could wet my pants, my bladder made me rush towards the toilet. I had goosebumps all over me and there was sweat running down my neck. The blood in my hands had dried off. I stood there thinking what should be done next. I walked over to wash my hands and looked at myself in the mirror. Mirrors are no less scary. They always make you see the unexpected, especially when the real picture outside the toilet is already haunting. I jerked off my hands and returned to the mirror. *This isn't real, this isn't real.*

I looked back in the mirror. I thought I saw someone in it, standing right behind me. My heart was beating fast and if I really saw someone there, it probably would have stopped. I returned to wiping my hands and turning away, but just then I felt something moving behind me in the mirror. I turned back with a start and the next instant there was a power cut. I screamed and ran towards the door when I realized that I was not the only one screaming in there.

I reached at the door knob when I felt someone's hands on mine. I was right; there was someone else. I nudged the person away while struggling to unlock the door and got out. The bathroom door was locked from outside and the person kept banging on the door from the inside. It was all dark around. A little light fell in from outside the windows.

I had no clue what was going around me. Inside my bedroom there was a lady moving on an easy chair and outside was a man waiting to get at me, and in my bathroom was another person – who could possibly be the one behind the bloodshed.

I stepped back and settled down in one corner of my living room. I don't know when I fell asleep.

My eyes opened up to the sunlight coming from outside. I lay in one corner of the room, seated with my legs crossed. My head was exploding with a terrible headache. I was covered in sweat. Like any other day, I walked up to the washroom scratching my butt, eyes half shut. I was completely oblivious of what had happened the previous night.

Squeezing the tooth paste tube, I opened my eyes to the mirror and put the brush inside my mouth. I spat and went back looking into the mirror and looked into it for a while. I suddenly remembered standing at the same place. Suddenly I recalled all the events of the previous night. I turned around to look for the man whom I had locked inside. The dividing curtain was scrolled aside and there he was, lying naked on the floor. I bent down to turn him around to face me and for once I thought that the universe was kidding with me.

It was none other but Mutthu, my servant.

It turns out that Mutthu never left the place. Every weekend, when I would never show up before nine at night on a Sunday evening, Mutthu would party at my place and brought home some girls as well. Unfortunately, I was home all weekend this time. By the time Mutthu discovered that I was home, he had taken off his clothes already and was in my room. With a girl.

Mutthu Swami, the dark, hefty, six feet tall lad who was good at doing nothing but blabbering in Tamil, spelled out his favorite word first after opening his eyes on the floor of my bathroom, "Ayyo!"

He said the same when he heard the door being unlocked and heard me enter the house as he lay naked on my bed, "Ayyo! Sir is home."

He stood up in haste and threw their clothes outside the window and left the window open. Before he could realize that there was a girl wearing nothing lying beside him, I was already in the foyer. He wrapped his girlfriend in the bedsheet that she was under a minute back and asked her to hide under the bed. Meanwhile, Mutthu sneaked out to check on me while I was in the kitchen and when he saw me going towards the couch in the living room, he ran inside the washroom and hid.

The girl fell asleep waiting for a perfect moment to get out. As the day grew grey and it thundered outside, she walked out and tried to fetch her clothes down the window when she slipped down from the table and the glass fell off the table and broke.

That was the banging window I heard in the first place. She started bleeding from a cut from a piece of the glass. That explained the blood on the glass and on my thumb later.

When she heard me coming into the room, she draped herself back, pulling the sheet to one side and hid under the table.

"So, she was the lady in white, bleeding on the easy chair. I get it now," I grinned at Mutthu sitting naked on the toilet seat as he narrated the whole story.

"Wait a minute, who was the man knocking at my door all night? He kept saying his wife is inside... one second, no! Don't tell me he was her husband!"

"Apparently yes," Mutthu replied.

"But, he looked really old!"

"Why do you think she was here?" he smirked at me, pulling up his virtual collar.

When the girl heard her husband banging on the door outside she was terrified and tried making a run for it from the window. At that moment I walked in to get the charger. She got no time to hide herself so she stuck to the wall and when I turned away from that wall, she sat down on the easy chair.

The man outside left after knocking for a while. He must have thought I was the one with whom his wife was sleeping. I reprimanded Mutthu by making him talk to me in Hindi for a month; it got pretty good by the beginning of the coming month. No girl was allowed to be brought home, not even the ones whom I wanted to sleep with. I considered it a double job to first get the girl and then send her off without leaving her tooth brush back at my place. And after having the old man knocking my heart beats away the other night – I would say triple trouble!

The next weekend while I was home, Mutthu and I shared beer over a decent non-scary movie and we made sure all the windows were locked this time.

Car No. 88

11th August 2014
8.00 a.m.
Char Bangla, Andheri West, Mumbai

It was a dark morning at the opulent white Raheja Villa. An unmarked police Jeep along with an ambulance had arrived under the porch of the villa. Two ward boys got down from the ambulance. They went in through the back door and within a few minutes brought out a body on the stretcher covered under a white sheet. At the entrance two constables were speaking to Mr Raheja, though they could barely draw out any meaning from his words. I stood at one corner watching the brunt of my own deed, and even though everyone mourned the loss, it all appeared to me a silent chaos. I could see everything happening right in front of my eyes, but it was as good as watching a film. I couldn't feel a thing. It didn't seem real; I wish it wasn't. But some things in life just happen; whether we wish it or not, whether we expect them or not. And this was one of those. I had killed my friend and whether I wished or not, I was a part of this movie; a very important one in fact.

The sub-inspector turned to me, "We may need you to come with us to the police station. Your friend is yet not in a condition to tell us anything. You are the only one who can help here, kindly cooperate."

Rakesh and I followed him to the station and even though now we were not part of the scene, it never stopped being a part of us. We couldn't stop thinking of Mrs Raheja who had lost consciousness, Mr Raheja's silence, the eyes of the sisters, the bare body visible from the corners of the bed sheet and the smiling face of Gourav that would be the hardest not to think about.

10.00 a.m.
Andheri West Police Station, Mumbai

"The person driving the car is in the hospital and in a critical condition. We are not sure when we'll be permitted to see him," the sub-inspector reported to his senior.

White coloured i20 it is with a VIP number 88. The left side of the car is wrecked. It's in our custody.

The constables could be heard discussing the case.

It is a clear case of drinking and driveing. Young blood, wants thrills – but don't know the limit.

So you know the limit when you want the thrill... they chuckled among themselves. *I may have to get a confirmation from your wife about that...*

"I guess we have heard you, Danish, and fortunately, you are not under the scanner. But I am afraid your friend in the hospital may have to report to us as soon as he gets back. You may leave now and just thank God that you are safe – from a lot of trouble," the sub-inspector said as he turned to us.

"Yes sir," Rakesh and I replied in unison.

"I hope you have learnt your lesson; and do not leave the city until the investigation is over," he added.

Rakesh and I rode back to the hospital to take a look at Anurag. The doctors said he was serious, serious enough to be worried about. He was put in the intensive care unit, under observation for twenty-four hours. He could be seen through the glass of the ICU. One of us was under observation by the doctors and the police, one of us was under a white sheet, and we, the remaining two had no idea about what had happened in the past eight hours.

The last thing I remember was the four of us – Anurag, Rakesh, Gourav and I, Danish – inside the car. The scene kept flashing in front of me how we teased Gourav all the time. Geeky Gourav, as we called him, because of his nerdy face behind the – 6.25 glasses. He was not a bookman, but a techie. The five-feet-seven-inches tall gadget geek was teased by everyone in college, but nothing, not even a warning from a lecturer to fail him in the finals for having not done the assignment, would take away the smile off his face.

Rakesh and I seated ourselves on a hospital bench outside the ICU. Our shirts were covered in dirt. There were tiny spots of blood all over. Rakesh had an injury on the left side of his torso and his palm was wrapped in gauge. There was the smell of blood and Betadine all over us, but it didn't stink as much as our souls.

I asked Rakesh about the time of the cremation. "Evening; around four," he replied folding his right leg up on the seat. We didn't share a word with each other after that.

10 August
Y.N. Institute of Management, Mumbai

In the midst of couples tweeting in the corners of the campus, girls of event organizing committees roared at their colleagues for the delay in sending out the invitations. The future Ambanis were busy meeting assignment dates; we, on the other hand, were planning out the weekend extravaganza.

"Don't spoil the plan, Gourav. We have been planning this all week long, where was your mommy then?" Anurag turned tapping Gourav's occipital.

"In Satna; Mommy was in Satna then. I had no idea she would be returning this weekend. She won't let me go out tonight. Not possible for me," Gourav said.

"Why are you such a spoilsport always?" Rakesh said, "At least ask her once. You never know, you might get permission," he added.

"Exactly! Why are you turning us down right away? We'll ask her. In the name of the last party before the exams," Anurag reasoned.

I was listening to their interlocution from one corner and slapped Gourav on the head. "Why are you so scared? Relax , we will take care of you. And in case your mother gets suspicious, we will ask Shreya to join us to baby sit you," I said giving Anurag a high five.

"It's nothing like that, you know it. My parents just don't approve of me staying out till late in the night. Once in a month it's fine, but..." Gourav intruded adjusting his glasses over his nose.

"...so this would be that once. Last time you weren't out late at night, rather were at Danish's place for the assignment.

Remember? You just be ready, we'll talk to your mom," interrupted Anurag.

"But..."

"Shush! We'll be there at ten. Be ready," Anurag snapped at Gourav.

"You people will really get me into trouble one day," Gourav said and shook his head.

"Don't you worry; we will be the ones to get your ass out of that trouble as well," I laughed, "and don't worry, we will let Shreya have a hand at it too." I chuckled.

We finally succeeded in getting Gourav to join us. Soon, the four of us were on the dance floor partying.

One shot after another, we all got drunk that night. It was a stag night and we went all out. Gourav was quite sober compared to the rest of us. He had to report home soon. Two shots later, he sneaked out while we were still at our game.

Three of us were pretty much single, except for Rakesh, who was not exactly a swimmer in the relationship pool, but did float in the shallow ones. He made his way, his hand around his girlfriend's waist. Gourav took his favourite corner seat and was soon lost in his cell phone.

We kept turning our eyes at the chicks around us, but at one point our sight was obtruded by a plump broad woman in a black dress who was seated alone. I turned to Anurag and gestured to him to check her out. It was just her at the table. She took sips of her drink and looked around once in a while. I got up to make my move. Before I could take a step forward, I realized the girl was looking at someone towards her right. Right there was seated my friend Gourav, who was making eye contact with her every five seconds. That bastard was finally getting some action, or reaction. We enjoyed their mute communiqué from the bar until the broad moved towards Gourav's couch to share a few words after the silent film.

Anurag and I went back to our glasses. In a while the big guy came back to us with the girl's number. We called for a bottoms-up. For the geek finally managed to lose his flirt-*ginity* – his virginity to flirt with a girl. The party went on for a few more hours.

2.00 a.m.

The bars were shut and we were on our way back home. Anurag took to driving that night. I sat beside him, while Gourav and Rakesh sat at the back seat. Gourav got busy texting the girl from the pub. He was very happy that night. The music was loud but the accelerator was under control. We were four kilometres from Gourav's place, humming the song on the radio.

Suhana safar aur ye mausam haseen...

We sung in symphony and it got louder. Suddenly, in the middle of the empty road, a bike headed our way. We honked. The biker tried racing after us. In no time the race turned into a fierce bout and both of our vehicles chased each other, speed matching speed to match our egos. Anurag and I were hell bent on winning the race and so we continued the game.

Rakesh and Gourav discouraged us, but we were too instigated to take them seriously; probably too drunk. Anurag eventually took his foot off the accelerator, but before it reached the brakes, the bike came in front of the car. The steering veered to the left and we climbed over the footpath. The car hit a tree ahead and turned upside down. It turned twice on its own axis and by the time we made any sense of what had happened, it was all over.

The car was upside down, there was absolute silence and all I could see in front of me was a fallen tree. I struggled and managed to get out of the car and called out the names of the others. Anurag was groaning on the other side. I helped him out of his seat. The car was a wreck.

I ran on the other side to pull Gourav out of the car. I could barely get my arm to reach him. I called out to Gourav, pulling him towards myself, when I fell back with his arm in my hands. His shoulder was smashed and so was most of the left side of his body.

♦

I never knew that carrying him then would lead to me carrying his body at his funeral a few hours later. After the cremation, we headed back to our homes.

5.40 p.m.

It seemed like a long never-ending period from the time of accident till now.

The building didn't sound noisy as always. I entered my apartment, locked the door and reached the refrigerator to grab a water bottle. My head was heavy. I sat down. The table in front looked dirty to me. I wiped it with my cuffs and swirled in a mouthful of water. It was too quiet around me. I looked at the clock in front of me. It was six in the evening and there was still time for me to call it a day. Six hours were left before I could go to bed and then all the turmoil would be over.

The body was in my arms when I pulled it out of the car – it didn't look like Gourav at all. One side of the face appeared to have never existed. There was blood all over. I shook him – again, then again, until I was shaking 'it', but there was no response. I don't know if he could hear me or see me, for his eyes were not visible to me. A part of his head was extirpated and a part of his skull was touching my thumb while I carried him to the hospital.

The bottle cap had dirt in its inner edges. I wiped it and turned back to the clock: the hands hadn't changed their position. The cap still looked dirty. I went to the kitchen to rinse it off. There were glasses in the sink. Suddenly I got an urge to clean everything. I washed the glasses, then the bowls near them, then the spoons from the rack, the plates from the shelf and every single utensil in the kitchen. Yet, they didn't look clean enough. My hands. The dirty hands couldn't wash away the dirt on the utensils; the cuffs on my wrist, the sleeves above them and my shirt. I pulled it off immediately and ran to the bathroom. I stood under the shower washing away the blood and the mud covering my skin along with the pain. I knelt down in the shower, breaking into tears and mourned. *What have I done!*

Anurag recovered soon and the charges were taken back by the Raheja family, for he was already facing the consequences. He would have a limp for life.

But even if we were charged and punished, what would have changed. Nothing could ever compensate for the loss.

The number 88 i20 still stands outside the Andheri Police Station, and can be seen every time we pass by.

I gave up drinking after that day. I learned the value of life. It is worth so much more than the pleasure of a few hours.

Drink, but don't get drunk.

(Inspired by a true story)